Terminalian Drift

Terminalian Drift

Jerry Gordon

Triarchy Press

Published in this first edition in 2021 by:

Triarchy Press
Axminster, UK
www.triarchypress.net

A catalogue record for this book is available from the British Library.

ISBNs:
Print: 978-1-913743-40-6
ePub: 978-1-913743-41-3
PDF: 978-1-913743-42-0

Printed by TJ Books Limited, Cornwall, UK

Special thanks to
Matt Azizi, Rie Hase and Pamela Mellott

1

I was out on the streets trying to get used to a new skin.

It was February 23rd. Morning. I walked down Midosuji Boulevard and into the heart of Osaka City. I was carrying a thin stick and trying to make things right inside. Or, more accurately, I was trying to adjust uncomfortable conflicts going on between my insides and an exterior surface I'd recently started living in.

A new skin commonly takes some getting used to. It's expected. But André Cadere's skin had been feeling way too tight. Way too restrictive. Way too unwelcoming. So, I needed to change things a bit.

To be more precise, André Cadere's skin was pinching the edges of my skeleton. My heels and hips, shoulders and wrists all felt like pointy points inside. The skin still seemed to belong to him. His skin tweaked me here and there. It was too taut at my corners and bony protrusions. The top of my head felt constantly pushed down by his shorter throat, and that compressed my spine. I couldn't turn my head or look up well. Gullet-grip kept my head slightly tilted over. Continuously bowed. Or, so it felt—like I was always dipping under some doorway.

It was obvious that my arms are longer than his were, so his skin felt bindy around the elbows. Things didn't bend quite right. There was no flexible flow. The skin didn't let me reach and twist in ways I was used to. Parts of it were too thick where I needed thin, or something like that.

But, all of that wasn't really such a big deal. Temporary misfits are pretty normal in a new skin, and I knew I could accept them.

But, the way his face restricted my jaw from moving was much tougher to get used to. I couldn't just get over that.

The face is always the center of attention, both from the outside and from within. The face couldn't be ignored. Talking, chewing, laughing and swallowing all became too self-obvious and kept reminding me of stuff I shouldn't need to remember.

Yeah, the wrongness of Cadere's face was what really got to me. That's what sent me into the streets.

2

Of course, like I said, a used skin comes with some issues. The differences between a skin I change into and the one I change out of always feel irritating and bothersome in the beginning. Little things irritate and make me doubt the choice to change, at least until a bit of my sweat and scent start to soak in and territorialize the new.

It's normal.

It's normal that I need to bring the former owner's claims on the skin to a more clear, or at least more believable, termination.

"Evict the ghost," as it were. Make the other mine.

And that was my goal for going into the city on that February day. That's why I was walking the streets and drifting around lost. I was hoping to alter my relationship with the new skin. I was hoping to suspend its previously established arrangements.

The start of something needs the ends of others. It's a basic and essential violence that existence survives on. It's something that we can't not live with. Live through. From condition to condition to condition, being goes from there to here, from there to here, from there to here.

A breath churns the air. A seed breaks—to open, to release a sprout, to start a tree. A sandwich kills a chicken.

It's an ecstatic temporality, but, it's also a process. Never a one time and finished deal. Not some kind of bim-bam-boom and done. It's about degrees of alteration and a variety of arrivals.

There's never any destinations along the way. Points of reference, sure, but not some big eventual. Stuff just keeps on keepin' on.

And while some starts and ends in life can be marked by crossing a distinct physical line, wearing a new skin is more vague. Less definitive. More destabilizing. It's hard to know when a skin really becomes mine. I don't think I can say any of them have ever really been me.

But that's not what I'm into changing skins for. If I was averse to unpredictability, I'd just have stayed in the skin I was born with. I like the dynamics of this practice, even when I don't like them.

But, too much discomfort is just too much.

It's not unreasonable for me to want to feel at home in a skin, or at least not feel like I'm constantly under the threat of eviction. I have a right to push back and press out. I have a right to shape what contains me. Maybe it's even a duty. And from my experience over the years, part of the process of getting placed well inside a new skin involves heat and getting the skin to a point of a fitting flexibility.

Of feeling fitting, flexibly.

Walking can help work things out.

When a skin fits, I can be less self-conscious about the mundane stuff. I don't need to think about turning a door knob or how my feet are placed beneath a chair. I don't need to think each detail when using a fork or lifting a glass of water to my lips. When the noticeable goes unnoticed, that's when I feel I've come to belong in a skin.

This sense of belonging definitely happens from the skin physically changing. Adjusting. Becoming more supple, flowing and pliable on my muscles, bones, joints, etc. It comes when the skin starts working with my habits of gesture. When it fits my movements.

But, it's also about me changing.

A new skin makes me lose something inside. Makes me work with unknowns. Makes me become a bit other.

And that is a big part of why I do all this. It makes me become something else.

3

Histories either require upkeep or erosion, depending on which way you hope they go. Histories are layered and fitted together in ways that even if you remove some pieces, the shapes of absent parts pretty much make things that are gone still there. Traces hint at what's missing. You can't just cut out part of something and expect the whole to knit itself together as a seamless new. The gaps are always part of the whole.

It's true everywhere.

Things removed leave traces. Bits of gluey residue from a sticker torn off a painted street pole still hint at the missing sticker's shape. A skin graft informs about its source: that it came from an ass or a shin or the nape of a neck. Faded spots on a jacket tell how the wearer moves, sits, uses the pockets or lugs a bag slung over the left shoulder. Such details indicate and hint at what was or what happened. Details whisper their history like ghosts. They haunt.

And if details point at something that has been blanked out or erased, those departed ghosts can keep on muttering.

And, I like those missing mutterings. I like hearing from the ghosts of skins.

When I am looking into getting a new skin, I imagine the voices of those ghosts. I imagine what they might be able to say. I imagine how much they might accent my voice if I live with them for a while.

But, until I can break a skin in—after my own personal processes of wear and tear infiltrate the skin enough times—the flesh remains a bit too haunted with its previous history. The ghost stays too possessive. Too roommatey. At such times, a skin gets a bit too co-residential.

That's not something to be unexpected, but it's not easy to live with either.

A used skin is rich with references. A skin always comes with traces that allude to its earlier behaviors, habits, likes, traumas, addictions, triggers, etc.

Other energies. Other's energies.

And, honestly, I deeply value those. I like that random abundance. Those urges. The beats of unknown pulses. The invisible density of inherited patterns and entangled ways. Marks marking the present with the past.

The presence of the past.

Callouses on a skin, for example, might show how much the person who had the skin before me worked with their hands. But more specifically I can tell if they were a guitarist, fisherman, nail biter, smoker or cook. Each person is always many things. And at different times. Selves layer. They pile up. And the body keeps track of them, marking those selves' moments and durations. Wrinkles and muscles of special use. Unique skills and lacks. Blemishes, dents and deformations. Affective aspects.

Scars become readable, like captions of childhood falls, violent brawls, a disease's crawl or periodic desires to end it all.

Each texture of scarring has a different script or intensity in its etch. A wriggled wad of tissue at the knee. Glowing thin streaks up the left wrist. A slice-line straight and white across a thigh that refuses to ever feel anything again. Such traces are a big part of why I like wearing used skins. I can get into them. They have echoes of hidden times that are both mysterious enough and hinting enough to keep me interested. They reveal their stories over time. Slowly releasing sequences, secrets, logics and effects. Skins have timings of a potential real.

They contain disembodied narratives that I get to imagine and piece together.

And during this imagining period, I think about how the story of the skin might have unfolded. I weave speculative stories from the plot points left by the scars' marks.

I fill in the blanks with maybes.

A slashing groove near the heart is maybe from...

A cigarette burn under the left foot is maybe from...

A forehead covered with angular digs is maybe from...

A rough patch on the inner thigh is maybe from scratching which is maybe from...

All are the aesthetic textures of a life in the first person, of a body's intimate contact with moments, spaces and contexts.

Wearing someone else's skin gives me a necessary distance to reflect on what is and isn't the evidence of a life.

Sure, the other wraps me uncomfortably for a while. But, after that, I can inhabit the other. I can make it mine. Make me it. Or, make it a me.

Then, rather than a container, a skin becomes a vehicle. A fleshy spaceship with time-travel options.

Towards what, I don't know or care.

Destination never.

And I had thought that André Cadere's skin would be a natural fit for me. A good fit. From what I'd read, I mean. About his life, I mean. About his art and how it was not really just about those sticks, I mean. That the sticks were a means. Levers to pry open worlds, I mean.

And that's why I finally bought the Cadere skin.

After coming across it in a search, I'd kept the skin marked on my Amazon *Wish List* for more than a month. As with most skins secretly traded nowadays, the Cadere skin was posted in the Hobby Department under the coded search-term: "*u*s*e*d*c*o*s*t*u*m*e*". Described as "Cadere André, 20/C, European Concept Art, Minor Renown." I researched about Cadere's career and became intrigued. Then interested. Then fascinated. Then committed. I compulsively checked if his skin was still available during that month of making up my mind. During that time, I imagined my life in him, as him, via him. Then, of course, I bought it.

It was delivered a few weeks later after being mailed through a series of obscure transfers. That's why the shipping costs were close to 50% of the price. The skin came wrapped in bubble-plastic inside a large box originally used for an Audio-Technica Belt-Drive Turntable.

Most of my imaginings in the two months before getting the Cadere skin were unrealistic. That is always true of the mythologizing stage of the process.

I knew the reality in the skin would not be what I fantasized. I knew it would be unpredictable. But I wasn't ready for how much. I wasn't ready for how far off I was. The actual experience of being in his skin was going too differently than I'd envisioned it would, or it should.

Expectations often give reality its bitchy side.

Or, I had simply forgotten the realities of what the process of wearing a new skin really entails.

Were things just imperfect or was I impatient? Probably, a lot of both.

So, basically, on the February 23rd morning I'm writing about, I was still feeling more confused than I thought I should. More confounded. More uncomfortable. Not a happy new-skin camper.

By February 23rd, the discomfort in Cadere's skin was more than I expected it should be at that stage in taking a new skin. The process was not feeling right, and so I was looking for a solution. A cure. I wanted a way out without leaving the skin.

And, so, I thought some drugs might help.

That's the reason why I was out on the streets in Osaka on such a winter's day. I was looking to adjust my system with some soon-to-expire medications.

I was out on the streets to score some randomizing agents.

4

Traditionally in Osaka, the drugs have run perpendicular to the banks.

Midosuji—the main boulevard—is set north-south down the center of the city. Lined by ginkgo trees and their billions of fan-shaped leaves, six lanes of south-bound traffic move like oxygenated blood into the city's body.

Osaka is traditionally a merchant city, and Midosuji is where the biggest Japanese banks set their Osaka offices. Decorated with shimmer and symbols for gold, the bank buildings' glass and glossy stone walls replace much of the sky.

The banks' names, coded-colors and logos whisper like gods of promise, speculation and profit: Mizuho, MUFJ, Bank of Tokyo, SMBC, Rizona.

Suitably, every winter, Midosuji's broad sidewalks are carpeted in dazzling gold as the fallen ginkgo leaves pile up. Pedestrians walk beside the boulevard atop clouds of brilliant yellow glow. It makes for picturesque strolling.

The putrid stench of rotting ginkgo nuts hints that such greedy luxury contains pungent side-effects.

The drugs intersect east-west.

Crossing Midosuji Boulevard is Doshoumachi Street.

For hundreds of years, traditional medicine-makers have fired their fat, bronze stills along this road. Through the varying eras of emperors, feudal lords, social turmoil and political powers, the bulbous Doshoumachi kilns, grindstones and presses have bubbled, sung and clanged, working to extract essences, compounds, agents and oils from all manner of matter.

For generations, the Doshoumachi drug labs distilled healing properties from roots, barks, fibers, leaves and grasses, from flowers, stones, dews, ores and airs, from sinews, cartilages, secretions, horns and bones, from whiskers, skins, glands, tongues, beaks and claws, from shits and pisses, from tears and waxes, from bloods, sweats, furs, nails, musks and biles.

Every material and its agential affects had long ago already been considered and categorized in the Chinese tradition. The parts and the wholes. The ethereal and the ephemeral. The symbolic characteristics of behaviors and qualities. The curative potentials and powers of placebo.

Japan's apothecarists inherited that tradition.

The fearless gaze of a tiger's eye.

The fertile she-rabbit's ovary.

The fuck-happy roster's sperm.

The ever-erect stag's horn.

The curseful caw from the complaining crow's beak.

The angelic grace of a crane feather falling in poetry and lore.

The aggressive force of the bull's testicles.

The eternal patience of the cliff-clinging pine.

The protective longevity of the turtle's shell.

The loyalty of the dog's wagging tail.

The mysteriously entrapping look of the eye of the fox.

The regal autonomy of the spine of the cat.

Each quality was measured for a logic of potency through ingestion, inhalation or rub.

Teas.

Fumes.

Pills.

Oils.

Creams.

Scents.

Injections.

In the right way, an element could even do its healing via simply the aura of its humming proximity. Just living with an elephant tusk in the room could improve memory and/or physical strength and/or penis size.

So it was believed.

So it is still believed, by some.

The motivational totem.

Along Doshoumachi Street, concoctions were (and still are) brewed, ignited, stirred together to be sipped, soaked in, swallowed and rubbed over requisite skins.

Even the aesthetic storage, labelling, measurement, grinding, scooping and blending of elements into powders, teas, combustibles and ointments can add value to the apothecary's healing affects.

Power to the packaging. Context is content.

Alongside the mechanisms of molecules, the rites of magic have always danced.

5

Traditional medicine makers integrate the life lived by source materials into their drugs' curative powers. Similarly, used skins are layered with thoughts. What's done doesn't just go poof and vanish. Skins contain purpose-filled lives.

Bodily talents.

Rote nerve knowing.

Muscle memories and skin imaginings.

Elbow know-how.

Knee skills.

Etc.

And each thought layering the body has its own intensity. The body has its ways to carry time. Store time. Tell time.

For example, Cadere surely smoked.

His lips—still even now—retain the skills for controlling a cigarette while his hands are busy. While "our" hands are busy.

Tensions and timings in his lips that are attuned to gravity maintain a longing for those cigarette rhythms. He still has smoker-lips.

Cadere's skin's lips know how to purse and grip and fondle a butt. How to angle and lever the required torque. His lips yearn for it. Even though I don't smoke, I can feel the lips' know-how. If I give them an unlit Lark, I can feel that my thinking moves a sense-layer closer to Cadere's. I think things that I wouldn't think without the stick of tobacco dangling between my lips. The cigarette is held firm and moved from spot to spot beyond my thought. Beyond my ability. These skills in the lips enable certain modes of pondering. That's something I like from a used skin. I can think things I wouldn't in my own skin.

There are certain aesthetics born of holding a rolled leaf between your teeth.

As well, a new skin is full of momentary stories. They contain befores, durings and afters. Durations, instants and potential forevers. Prisons that trap within—and wings that enable flight from—impossible circumstances.

Skins are thinking entities. And they're willing to share some insights.

"But how to know how a skin is thinking?" you might ask.

While not generalizable, a body's thoughts are readable through aires of premonition and the body's readinesses to respond.

A skin's vibes sing its contact with traumas, revelations and joys.

Zeitgeist skins. Contextual flesh.

The body maps events within its flow through life. Via entangled senses. Blended feelings unique to their moment. Via storylines stored in wrists, waists, ankles and thighs. By noticing such ghosts of times-past, I can speculate about things a skin experienced in times before I got it.

Phantom calendar architecture.

For example, at some time in his life, Cadere was likely violently hit in the back by an object and knocked to the ground. The event traumatized him. I can also tell that, in response to the blow, he probably rolled away from the spot after crashing down onto the pavement, or maybe onto a patch of rough ground. He likely rolled away to escape the energy of the shove.

I conclude these invisible events because there is a dull point—about the size of the tip of a broom handle or a gun muzzle—just to the left of his right shoulder blade. His skin still contains the event. His skin still holds the duration of what happened, and also what was the lead-in and the finish of the traumatizing event.

The skin stores the event's choreography.

The skin holds the sensation of the point. And the point is connected to the feelings that came before and after. This all sets that point in his back within the flow of this skin's body-time.

That point on Cadere's back hums with anticipatory worry, hums of threat, hums of knowing that something would likely happen. And thus that point on this skin is still now wrought with caution's rigidity. His skin has an awkward readiness to respond without knowing what response to take.

Touching the spot right now, or even just bringing it to mind, sets off ripples through the skin's event-flesh. The spot knots together sensations of moments that preceded and followed the violent blow. Layers of history are enfolded backward and forward in time from the incident's physical contact with the body. The spot on the skin is infused with fear because of the violent punctuation of the blow.

The blow sent out ripples which gave meanings to moments before and after.

The blow informed moments with cause and effect.

The point still gives meaning. Still attaches to meaning. Still terrorizes with meaning.

Pasts are written by futures, and vice-versa.

The small round spot in Cadere's back orients particular events around itself. The events and their ordering give the spot a context within the various other histories that his body contains. The spot on this skin's back bristles with a vague anxiety. It anticipates violent possibilities.

In the same way, the point in Cadere's back stores what followed the push: Cadere's flailing tumble forward beyond his legs' ability to stay under his thrusted torso going past balanced and into gravity's abrasive tug.

When I think now about the spot in his/my back, I can also feel it igniting in his/my hands. They remember flashing out to grasp, block or cushion the coming crash. My palms remember the burning scraps that followed after the impact that rammed against his back and shoved him beyond his control and then down to the ground.

All these pains and sensations orient each other inside the process of the violence. They are the enshrined rite of trauma. They potentially bind being to it. As the skin's current occupant, I must take on a bit of this violent affect. I can't call it my experience, but it is mine.

It's of me because I must share it.

It's us stuff.

6

Freedom is an absence of links.

In a used skin, there are often bouts of memory seep. At times they're regular occurrences, and other times they are random floods of flashbacks that transfer the skin's experiences to the cognitive meat of me.

They are how the skin weaves a net of references.

Sensory hallucinations and mystery itch. Traces of incidents—a needle prick, punch in the gut or lazy caress—continue echoing in the flesh.

Across the gap between meat and skin, the past leaps with its hooks and strings, building a lattice of habits, urges, addictions and drives.

A skin offers its gifts and threats.

A skin tries to train my brain to its thousand churning hungers and wills. It tries to shape me to fit the world filtered by its surfaces. Those are its territorializing efforts, trying to shape how I should experience its form as I move inside it inside the world. The skin wants me to believe how it shapes the world's surfaces with its touch and step and sniff and lick. It wants me to believe in the way it includes me in its presumed totality. The skin wants me to believe it about how everything is, about how everything is OF it.

But, I can't just let a skin control shit.

I have to push back. I have to push out at its limits.

Thus, being in a new skin can definitely be kind of overwhelming.

A skin has its ways of making me fit its precursors. And Cadere's skin was exerting a lot of itself. More than I'd expected. More than I remembered should be expected. More than was normal in the skin trade.

I have learned to resist such assertions of the skin. To live with a skin, I have to keep the balance vibrant. I have to not lose too much of myself.

Just enough blurring is best.

Which one of us occupies the other has to become vague enough for a future to form beyond the mere perpetuation of habits and the "as always." Without that vague vibrancy, nothing creative can come about. Being in a skin has to be an improvised collaboration of mutual confusions, of strong desires making the new.

And so, I was out in Osaka City that February morning because I felt I needed to lightly suspend both the skin's senses and my own. I needed to facilitate our meeting in a mutually unanticipated space. Someplace between outside and inside.

I needed a drug-induced no-man's land. Some slightly foreign unsettled place of medicated senses. A slightly altered state.

So, that's why I was in the streets in that ill-fitting skin. Like a schizophrenic out for a walk, I was both trying to get more used to Cadere's proportions—sweat his skin up a bit and make it feel more right—but also looking to get a fair supply of random legal drugs.

7

You might ask, "Why legal drugs?"

The fact is, while every drug tweaks the system it enters, the potent and dramatic effects of illicit drugs make the system suspect its limits too much for my purposes. They create sensations and considerations that make the system question the fundamental normality of normality.

Hard drugs reflect the reflection found in a meta-logical mirror, making the user try to catch the mirror observing itself as observer.

Isn't that what "trippin" is all about?

Basically, illicit drugs give the feeling of having sure answers for which I don't know the questions. Fun and amazing, to be sure, but not my goals in this case. I was hoping to have the drugs moderate a new normality between the skin and me rather than throw out the whole idea of normality as mere fakery.

Regardless of its falseness, reality lets us live with others.

Thus, I was looking for the more subtle phase-shifts that are created by over-the-counter medications. Non-prescription drugs more softly disorient the body's default settings, re-instilling the body's state of tolerable pain rather than elation. After an aspirin, a headache gradually pounds less and less. The body then forgets why it needed the pain to begin with, such as for signaling some other ailment.

Kind of a bait-n-switch.

With non-prescription drugs there is no ecstasy of mind-expanding feel-good joy-joy. Just a return to common-place suffering.

I hoped that this type of slight alteration of the typical sensations for both Cadere's skin and myself would result in both sides of the divide more quickly orienting into a neutral normal, a less resistible mundane. I hoped we could get along and share a sense of a mutually derived co-territorialized space.

That's what I wanted, but I didn't want to choose what drugs I used.

I wanted randomness.

Using random drugs would prevent me from feeling I was directing the experience.

8

In the weeks after buying the skin online—as I waited for delivery—I felt excited and driven to make several Cadere-like sticks.

Before leaving my house on the morning of the 23rd, I stood in my chilly kitchen and looked at the five sticks I'd constructed.

They stood propped against the wall.

A dirty oblong clock slowly ticked above them. The second hand was faulty—always leaping toward second :47 before falling back to second :46—but the minute and hour hands kept good time.

The time was 9:13:46.

The colorfully banded sticks leaned stoically against the grey concrete wall. They seemed to mark the wall for length, measuring it with their varied sections of color.

None of the sticks strictly followed the aesthetic that Cadere had established in his work. Other than being longish and stick-like, they didn't look like Cadere's sticks at all.

He'd used round, painted blocks that were the same height as their diameter. Their thickness was their height was their depth. Cadere used various systems to decide the ordering of colors along his sticks' lengths. These systems even included intentional mistakes. Then, after the formula had decided the form of a particular stick, the colored blocks were assembled like beads into that stick. Some sticks were long. Some were short. Some were thick. Some were slender.

My sticks are more colorful, and I think mine are also better-looking.

Cadere would carry one of his sticks wherever he went, but it wasn't a walking stick. Never a cane, although plenty of people tried to reference that purpose. Others tried to interpret his work and say that he was like a shepherd for the passive lost sheep of the art world. But, he never admitted any purpose or referent for his sticks. He didn't even call them sticks. That's another reason why mine weren't his.

He called his sticks, "bars." And that kind of fits how much he drank and presented his works (and lectures on his works) in beer halls. His artwork was not restricted to gallery walls or other such exclusive spaces. His art was about opening, undermining, or even destroying such spaces. Everywhere was his exhibition space. Everywhere he went was his art's context.

I've only seen Cadere's sticks in photographs and a common way they're shown is leaning against gallery walls. A lone stick leans in the space, the rest of the room and people are oriented around it. The stick orients that world.

And such photos of Cadere's sticks have taught me things.

A stick leaning against a wall has a certain range of angles.

Too steep and the stick will fall over. Too shallow and it will just fall down. The angles that allow a stick to stay propped up convey a very direct logic. They show that the stick is either stable or pushing a limit, past which gravity will take over. If you see a leaning stick, you can feel when it's near to falling over or when it is firmly set and stable. The stick communicates that to us. We see it in its relation to gravity.

The leaning stick is something very important in Cadere's work, for me anyway. His works made a constant but unassuming reference to everything else that was giving them a context. His sticks were never without a setting. The power of his sticks was in how they shaped the setting around themselves. The sticks identified Cadere as Cadere when he carried one, but also when he didn't. A lone stick would indicate he was there. The sticks provided the context for who he was, and he could take that context with him, wherever.

He made the sticks and the sticks made him.

But settings also indicated the different pressures on the sticks, like the constant pull of gravity. Or, the otherness of someone else's artwork displayed beside a Cadere stick created the stick's role and identity. Cadere's work, like Cadere himself, was showing that it exists within conditions of stability and instability. The sticks show they are in dynamic collaboration with those conditions, regardless of whether the conditions are of struggle or conflict or cooperation or admiration or infiltration.

9

So before I left my house on that February morning, the sticks I made were leaning in my kitchen beneath my broken but accurate wall clock. I stood there staring at them and trying to choose which one to take with me into the streets of Osaka.

In contrast to Cadere's assembled bars, my five sticks were all just solid wooden sticks. I'd found them around the house. They weren't round blocks glued together in a programmed color pattern which included a programmed mistake. I just painted mine by inspiration using different colors of paint I had in a box. The patterns of my sticks were made of unequal-length sections of color, not following any system of integrated mistakes except for the ones that inherently bubble within me.

I painted them as the colors interested and attracted me, as the colors seemed to desire their place and their length and their neighbors along the stick.

I tried to not decide too much, which is probably the most programmed system there is in contemporary life. Try to be authentic. Just let shit be.

But, I have to say, I trust collaborating with objects. While probably no critic will ever see my sticks, if I was questioned about the logic of my aesthetic, I'd say that I let the colors and the sticks exert their desires.

How can I claim to be on collaborative parity with a piece of wood that I found in my backroom and some tiny tubes of paint left to me by an ex-girlfriend? I do it by accepting that the choices are not only mine. I do it by thinking the sticks deserve as much credit as me for how they turned out. They used me as much as I used them.

Whether that is anthropomorphism, animism or just dodging blame, I don't care. The sticks are not about my choices or my design. And, neither am I—I guess—regardless of the extents that I've gone to trade into some skin and out of others, to live in one place and not another, to be this or that but not something else. Where does authority or authenticity get stamped at any step in the process? When is the particular time that orients all the other times? By what or by who?

I don't know, but the questioning always interests me.

Anyway, back to choosing from the sticks in my kitchen.

Three of the sticks were about a meter long. One was exactly my arm's length. The last one just came up to my knee. None of the sticks were round. All were thin, with their four sides aligned on differing angles, like acute trapezoids.

After probably too much internal deliberation, I took one of the long sticks. Time had run out for considering. It was 9:19:46 and my train would leave at 9:26. I chose, left my house and started walking. It felt awkward at first to be out on the street with a striped stick. Like I was carrying a tapping cane for the heretical blind. I felt self-conscious.

While walking with the stick was partly a nod to any physical programming Cadere's skin might still have in relation to carrying a stick, I also did it as a would-be habit. My project was to embody him. I wanted the action which had identified Cadere to become usual for me and to thereby discover what would come about from it. How would the stick determine my movements, speed and feel in motion? How would carrying a stick affect my capacities to think in the skin? What would I lose and gain?

I once read, if you want to live someone's life, you should steal that person's groceries and eat their choices for a week.

I was looking to trace the effects of Cadere's comparable details.

I caught the Loop Line train to Osaka station and then headed toward Midosuji on foot.

10

I walked down Midosuji carrying my chosen stick. All the gold leaves were gone and the street was lined by bare trees.

I listened to the city's minuscule voices coming from close and far, blending into a song made up mostly of whispers. Sibilant drifts of sound wrapped my head. Within this mix, I heard an isolated sound exiting from a side street. Something thin and lost.

Up a very narrow street between the faces of two tall bank buildings, a lone man stood with a saxophone. But he wasn't making city-saxophone-man sounds.

Seeing a man with a sax on a city street makes me expect blasts of jazz melodies, tones and phrases that place themselves up within the windowed skies of office buildings and assertively orient the city's other sounds in contrast to unique shapes of blown musical flows.

But this guy was playing different. I can't call it "his" sound. He was playing something more frailly derived from within the city's own textures. He was playing in collaboration with the city's random thrusts.

I walked into this canyon of buildings.

As I approached, I could see that the man was obviously playing, but I couldn't hear anything. Or, I didn't know how to hear anymore.

Then, when I got closer, I could pick up some sounds, but I couldn't find any melodic flow to follow. At times, sparks of tone and texture would reach far enough up the street for me to hear. But, at other times, his fingers' movements were my only hint I got that sound was occurring.

I watched and let my listening reach out. But it didn't feel like I was getting everything, if in fact there was anything to get.

I drifted closer. I stopped and stooped down at a spot directly across the narrow car path dividing my side from the saxophonist's. My striped stick touched the sidewalk slab like a tool to catch vibrating textures that might guide me through deafness.

It kind of worked. I started to sense what I sense he was doing.

He was playing with the city from within the city. He was responding to the sounds approaching him at that precise location. He was playing with the metropolis's million disparate voices bouncing off urban surfaces and arriving at his spot.

This point.

His center of the city.

And into these murmurs of the city, he was slipping his own varied voices.

But he made an effort to not overload the others. He didn't want to make his own sound a focus of more attention than the others shaping the space where he was listening. He was not playing to an audience greater than himself and the other participant sounds.

He was letting his listening continue to gather in the textures becoming present.

Perhaps in a hope to hear his own heart beat within the city's pulse, as a shared urge of sound-blood in flow, he gave all the city's contaminant elements fair respect.

At times, his sound would vanish before it could reach all the way across the street to me. His sound would trail off into an embrace with some growing city volume that took over the space or washed his sound out.

Later, my hearing slightly shifted to focus on machine noises drifting in from the city, and then I noticed that there was an overlaying happening from his horn. There was some reply or partial duplication he was smuggling into the city's folds. As the city's sound would phase out, the saxophone might carry that tone of the city beyond the city's making, stretching a noise or texture out farther than the city could maintain it alone.

The time of the timely in league with the artifice of expression.

The voice in echo recharged with a desire to go on longer than urban nature has power to let it live.

A squeak.

A rattle.

A peeling slide of pressures in decay.

And then at different points, the pure tone of utter human manufactured sound grew and blasted forth. A sound from the city would arrive and get a parasite of human art burrowing itself into it. And then the saxophone sound would rise up and up and up in the kind of power and abrasive thrust that is human expression saying, "I am here after all and fuck you if you don't acknowledge my pride."

I'm sure the experience that the man was having was different from mine. Him listening from his position and perspective versus me squatting four meters away across the street holding a thin wooden stick that was trembling slightly.

This was my wholly distinct center. His was his.

But, it seems too that that would be part of the point. Part of his point.

My center cannot be his, but neither of our ears is superior. Neither damages the other's auralation.

Even his playing and his listening were not the same thing. The sounds coming to him from the city and the sounds coming from his horn, all along their various points of resonance, surely form a singular and particular expression that is relative to his hearing.

And mine is the same but different.

The two of us could perhaps share the fact that we shared degrees of this difference, or that we differed in shared ways, or that we shared interests in being different.

He came to an end of playing.

I watched him unhook the saxophone from his neck strap and squat down to set the instrument on one of the black/yellow striped concrete curb stones that ran the length of the small street. The contrast of shiny metal and painted concrete seemed like a new gesture, some act of rebalance.

The name "Marsyas" was engraved into the brass and showed signs of a greenish rust.

He looked at me and pointed. He said something I couldn't hear, but I assumed it was about the colorfully-banded stick I was carrying. The city's sounds had flowed between us loud enough to scramble his voice, but his finger's movements in the air conveyed: "striped colors." I nodded and held the stick up like I knew what he meant.

We both moved into the street and met halfway between.

"Not for blindness?"

"Huh?" I awkwardly figured. "Oh, no. It's for nothing really."

"Nothing too real works best."

"I agree."

"You just out walking?"

"Yeah, and to the parade."

"Medicine one on Doshoumachi? Yeah, that's today, isn't it?"

"How long you playing?"

"Maybe once or twice more."

"Enjoy it."

"It's not really about enjoyment, but I will. Oh, are they still throwing drugs out at the parade?"

"I hope so. That's why I'm going."

"Enjoy it."

"Haha. Yeah, likewise."

I waved good-bye and moved back towards Midosuji. The golden saxophone stayed calmly perched on the black and yellow concrete curb. Like silence resting on a tiger's back.

I turned south and headed the few blocks further toward Doshoumachi.

11

Outside of a café just ahead of me, I watched a worker throw a bucket of water out across a patch of granite sidewalk, and the water remarked.

It marked the dry ground. It marked the energies of direction and reach. It marked gravity and atmospheric pack. It came to a pooling pause, but it didn't stop. The water seeped and evaporated: down into the earth's pull of porous interstices and out into skies.

Water only knows how to flow. It never ceases. Even glaciers thousands of years old are not a stilling of water. A chilling, but not a stilling.

The city is likewise, imposing its own flows of seep and sink and evaporation.

Streets maintain ancient lines made of desired moments, those occurring again and again. Repeated choices are conveyed as a compiled logic onto the streets' current users, a logic that cannot be determined by, or sourced in, any politics other than a sense held in common. It is a logic born of stereo-optic vision, of fingernails, of the gooey tube running through us from mouth to anus, of of of, etc.

A city exists with a priori contexts that are placed on bodies moving down or up a hill. A city is its people against or with a wind that gusts between buildings that have replaced buildings. A city exists on the light that stirs amidst its layered angles of shadows.

This is not a commonsense.

Not a culture of a time.

It's a sense that peoples of remote eras learn from the city's questions, from confluences of place and urge.

Lowest spot between here and there.

Highest line of sight.

The best way around whatever permanences maintain.

The view that includes how much of what was seen by others.

A place's sources of purpose: access water, direct wind, align to light, find protection.

And the new.

12

Japan's pharmaceutical industry has now mostly evolved beyond its origins in traditional Chinese medicine. Some of the snake oils and turtle teas and armadillo-dung pellets are still made and sold, but those traditions are looked upon with a little more derision and a little less attraction.

And, while the medicine industry has tried to shift its image to that of a high-tech agent of the scientific method, drug makers in Osaka don't forget their ancient background.

Tradition runs strong here. Thus, each year on Doshoumachi Street, there is a parade via which the history and blessings of the medicine-makers are remembered through thematically decorated floats and marchers.

Starting at 10am, the parade sets off from Sukuna-Hikona shrine and proceeds due west until the street dead-ends where one of the city's ancient water canals has been filled in and replaced by an overhead highway.

The canal once brought boats into the heart of the city, boats carrying the raw materials from which the old medicines could be derived. The antelope heads and bottled mercury. The paper-enfolded powders of semens sourced from monkeys, storks, snakes, heroic soldiers and certain willing gods. Giraffe tails. Phoenix lungs. Bear stomachs. Leopard dongs.

Every kind of material that could be logicked to transmit improved health was transported into the heart of Osaka via the city's tangled system of canals.

Where the now-filled-in canal once flowed, Doshoumachi Street is now forced to end. And thus this is where the parade ends, and disbands.

Most of the floats that are carried aloft down the street are carefully placed into scented cedar containers and trucked back to the warehouse which will store them till next year. The others are smashed into a huge wad of broken sticks and crackling plastic before being tossed in a large metal trash box or just set on fire.

The parade is now held each year on February 23rd, corresponding to the ancient Roman end-of-year festival called Terminalia.

For hundreds of years, this parade down Osaka's medicine street took place on the afternoon of the day before the Chinese lunar new year. But around a century ago, the date was changed to follow the ancient Roman celebration for the god Terminus: the god of boundary markers, barriers and property lines. While it is vague and seemingly odd that an ancient Roman holiday was adopted by a local network of Osaka drug companies for their traditional event commemorating the history of their industry, there is a plausible story.

And I know this story. Sort of.

I have asked around and have compiled something that kind of makes sense as a history. At least for me.

You can take it or leave it.

Or, check it to the degree you can and want to.   `

You can even add what you find.

Or, just trust me.

13

This is what I've come up with.

First of all, Terminalia kind of fits the theme of ending one year and transitioning to the new. Out with the old and starting fresh, etc. Also, people who claim to know say that Terminalia can also make sense with symbolically ending an illness and starting a period with renewed health. Life is laced with many such symbolic moments where ends are the start of new beginnings.

Those two reasons generally work as symbolic motives for why Osaka drug makers observe Terminalia. Those are what most people will tell you if you ask about it. But, those are almost the same symbolic reasons for staging the parade on the last day before Chinese New Years.

So, why the change to an Italian god?

I'll tell you.

My research has found some more entangled factors which come into play for why Terminalia is now the date for the parade. These are exclusively word of mouth histories, and I have not read any of them supported by experts. But, I am a fan of weaving speculative histories into the gaps for which we have no knowledge. So, I'll spread what I have collected from here and there. You can take them with as much cynical caution as you feel is appropriate.

From what I have put together so far, the origin of using Terminalia may have come from a popular interest in Italian culture that happened in Japan just after World War I. This popularity arose and lasted for a brief period around 1920. At that time, Italy had been one of the western nations that supported Japan's efforts to include a Racial Equality Clause in the Treaty of Versailles. With that clause, Japan hoped to fundamentally influence the rules governing the League of Nations and prevent racial bias.

Japan was the only non-western nation to fight with the allied forces against Germany in WWI, and at Versailles Japan made a proposal for equality between member countries without distinction for race or nationality. Japan's racial equality clause was inserted in the language of the treaty and it even won a majority of votes from the other participating countries. But the idea was rejected by Britain due to Australian colonial concerns. As a result of Britain's rejection, the majority vote was overturned by Woodrow Wilson.

In consolation, Japan was given possession of formerly controlled German territories in China and Polynesia.

Thus, in a time before the wave of nationalist militarism became officially entrenched in Japan, Italy's support for Japan's efforts with regard to equal human rights gave birth to a period of popular interest in Italian culture and various business exchanges. Italian food became popular, in particular *gelato*. Italian operas were performed. Images of *Roma* were hung on the walls of Italian-styled coffee shops.

It is said that this period of Japan's "Roma-Boom" is when an exchange between Osaka and Italian drug companies briefly flourished and when Dr. Archimede Menarini, the founder of Menarini Pharmaceuticals, made a visit to Osaka from Florence. His visit was supposed to occur at the same time as the Osaka group's annual lunar New Year's parade. But, because his ship was delayed in transit, the hosting Osaka medicine makers delayed the parade until his arrival. But, he didn't arrive until after Chinese New Year. Supposedly, Dr. Menarini informed his Osakan hosts about the February 23rd Roman festival of Terminalia during a drinking session following the dinner held in honor of his arrival.

The drunken energy of the party thus latched on to a new date for the drug parade, an updated and new orientation of a conclusion.

Sometimes when you are beyond the end, you find a new image of the end.

Thus, Terminalia.

So, while Japan's brief Italian fad may appear to be a culmination of random or unconnected energies, no moment is without traces. What might appear as random can be evidence of trajectories so complex that it is hard to determine any primary cause. Motivations and connections can occur from unseen, unnoticed or forgotten currents. They can arise from exhaustion with old historical directions as well as desires for transformational futures. And vice versa.

The thing that gets the chance to point is what sets the direction. Effects follow. This is true from shifts in sway to decision-making power access. It's true of winds and a ship's delay. It's true of an after-dinner drinking revel. It's true of overriding a vote, and a slap of disrespect. It's true of a fear of others having control, or even equality. It's true of giving a concessionary approval to colonial domination. Each element in a mix works in both predictable and unpredictable ways. It's hard to know how the world would have spun differently if the only non-western country to fight in WWI had been granted a single sentence promising racial equality rather than given the colonial control over peoples formerly controlled by Germany.

Who the fuck knows?

The minds of utopians and paranoids are equally filled with "What ifs?"

Regardless, and thus, Osaka's pharmaceutical companies hold their annual parade on Terminalia, February 23rd. Or so I've concluded.

And equally thus, I ventured down to Doshoumachi Street on that day to attend the parade and get me some free drugs. With them, I hoped to redial the recently embodied skin that was irritating the shit out of me. Or, I was irritating myself in it.

The miracle of each mundane moment.

14

But I have to say, this parade event isn't known by many people and information about it is not widely shared. In some ways, it's as though it doesn't even exist.

Even though the visual elements of the parade are beautiful and mysterious, the event is pretty much shunned by the media and general public. The few parents who know about it often forbid their children from attending. They view the parade as "dangerous" or "scary."

Actually, the parade's hidden and blotted-out aspects are much of what attract me to the event. I'm kind of that kind of obscurist.

But, I can understand the parents' concern. Because, in addition to commemorating the history of medicines, the drug companies distribute almost all of the previous year's left-over medicines to the onlookers. For free. They toss the drugs out onto Doshoumachi Street like candy. The event is a day when body-system modification tools fall to the ground like rain. A boon for all who either can't afford such drugs or who just want to scoop up—and collect—the colorfully packaged dead-stock.

Trash is treasure.

Of course, in our current age of protective legal responsibility, this kind of practice might appear dangerous. I guess it actually is. That image is why the event is largely ignored by most and shunned by some. But, while the dangers are possibly true, all these medicines are in fact legal and tested and can be bought by anyone. These are not prescription drugs. They're over-the-counter goods available at most any drug store or supermarket.

The fact is that the whole event to distribute the old drugs is part of a contract that the original medicine workshops made with the feudal powers that held sway in the past. It was part of the deal the medicine makers made in order to get permission to set up their first stills on Doshoumachi. The contemporary drug companies are just keeping that promise to the ancestors of their industry.

The medicine makers were told that they had to spread health freely to the public each year as a blessing from the rulers of society. Thus, the parade and open distribution of whatever drugs were made in the previous production run took and takes place. And each year is different. Some years there are mountains of athlete's foot creams. Other years, lots of cough drops. Ibuprofen capsules. Eye drops. Balding tonics. Condoms. Yeast infection powders. Fever pills. Energy drinks. Etc.

The surprise is part of what makes the event fun and exciting.

Skillful gatherers—or swappers—can save a lot of money, so there are usually a fair number of pensioners scrambling into the street to stock up on joint creams and pain killers. They often trade what they get for what they want.

But, for me, I went down to the event because of the randomness. That was my draw.

My hope was to collect a hoard of drugs that I knew nothing about and to then see if they could improve my life in the Cadere.

15

And maybe you've been wondering about something. Maybe you have been trying to imagine how someone puts on someone else's skin.

Well, getting into a used skin is no easy task.

The ideal situation would be to have help. As with most complex processes that deal with adjusting the body, it would be great to have professional help, or even a willing assistant. Some trustworthy other set of hands and eyes that can make the procedure easier. A person with special skills that he or she has developed to be of help in the shadows of society. I would love that kind of help, but I can rarely find it.

Also, working with someone would be a nice way to share the secret and the excitement. To have an assisting confidant.

Perhaps you are now imagining an Igor.

That wasn't really what I was thinking of as an assistant, but actually an Igor wouldn't be bad to have.

Some bent-bodied outcast from society who feels a duty to his Dr. Frankenstein would be a big help. Maybe the Igor has a personal passion in matters that the "greater" society shuns, banishes people for, or mobs with fire.

An Igor would likely know how to effectively swim against the social currents of whatever time or location he (or she) lives in. As the societal crowds feel driven to inflict normality on every aberration they identify, Igor slinks around out of their sight, maybe right beneath their noses.

As his name and accent divulge, he is a born outsider, perhaps on multiple levels. He fails at the tested orientations of Us-ness. Physically: odd. Culturally: odd. Criminally: odd. Surely psychologically: odd. Likely spiritually: odd.

What about ethically? It's hard to measure that. Because, while digging up recently buried bodies and putting the pieces together in another form are not sanctioned behaviors in any culture, burying the dead in the first place isn't a universal means of dealing with lifeless flesh. Dead animals, for example, are eaten. Actually, the edibility of animal meat is often the cause for not just their death but for their birth in the first place.

However, I get the point. People dispose of dead people, either underground, or up with smoke, or in a river, or to the birds. And people want the dead to stay dead. They want them to stay away.

I get it.

But, my point here is that an Igor likely has his own ethical qualities. He has a code of right and wrong. He's not eating recently departed grandmas or collecting trophies off of executed criminals. He just sees another option to death. Igor doesn't heel to the "dead is dead" idea that is most common. He sees a new chance in what the social group believes is an absolute end.

But, Igor doesn't confront them about it. He doesn't need to convert them. He doesn't want to give them his secrets or change the world. Igor stays quiet. He hides from the group and their mutually approved ideas. He keeps to his work and sneaks around so that society doesn't notice him or his actions. That way, he can eke out the life of his own vision.

He makes a life using what the wider society doesn't want to imagine. What it can't see.

He lives off what the mob discards and what its logic overlooks.

They bury the dead, as soon as possible. And, in that, Igor sees a huge waste. He sees life being lost. He sees potential being squandered.

Igor knows the dead are not dead yet. Not really dead. Not wholly dead.

He knows death has various degrees over time.

Igor thus knows he needs to get to a new gravesite as soon as possible after a burial. Igor has to get there before "God" gets a hold on the dead. Igor sees that death is a wasteful misperception of man. He sees other potentials and processes that remain open. At least for a while.

Igor sees that the rules God gives to man are not the only ones. Igor sees others.

Igor sees that God makes use of the dead too. God extends life. Igor sees that God plays by different rules, not much different from Igor's.

Both Igor and God fold the flesh of the dead back into the bodies of life. Of different life. They both perpetuate the miracle of animation. They know life has no expiration date, and death is more like a map than a destination.

Igor knows this. Death informs him of where things can go, not merely where they are. He knows how to adjust his perception in relation to shifting contexts. Igor knows death opens things up to new ways. Death opens things up to otherness. Death doesn't freeze something into some change-denying statue. Death isn't static. Death has a dynamic and flow. Death has a way with life.

Igor knows that the raw materials of life are willing. Sure, they will observe and fulfill human rituals of meaning. They will burn or embalm. The dead body will go along with those ideas. But Igor knows the body's bits are also obedient to other attractions. The stuff of us is open to becoming lost in a turbulence of categories. The flesh is open to differences. The body will willingly embrace rot and chemical drift. The flesh will willingly dance with micro-flora and fauna. The blood can blossom as the coagulated flowers of decay and the pungent neon glow of stink.

Igor knows there are a million-trillion possible trajectories opening and closing when a body's system lets down its guards, or rather switches its processes towards different developments. When the body's materials change direction, new maps become possible. And these maps of death are what Igor is learning how to read.

The body is open to entangling with others open to entangling. At death, the body's elements become available for creation, not just perpetuation of its systemic limits. At death, the body accepts offers of collaboration.

If you think it is amazing that the body can grow a toenail, you should also accept the miracle of gangrene's spread and the decomposition of sinew.

I don't know how any of these creative processes take place. Neither do you. But, Igor knows that one possible path for a "dead" body is to re-enter the human coil.

Igor has developed knowledge and skills. He knows how to sew flesh back in with flesh and jump-start a next round.

Igor is more humane than flies and worms. Matching and mixing viable bits, Igor seeks to reactivate breath, pulse, sense, thought and action. Igor—this bent human oddity who is judged as inhuman enough to deserve immolation—knows that there is no limit to the forms life can take.

Igor knows life is ceaselessly abundant.

Life creates itself, and in that ecstatic temporality life makes itself uncategorical.

Life makes itself its only fair measure.

That's the perfection Igor sees: something without comparison or a pre-cursor model to measure against.

Igor is not a Platonist. He's more of the "Judge not, lest ye be judged, Mutherfucker!" school.

Igor also knows he's in this almost alone, with even Dr. Frankenstein not really fathoming him.

Igor knows he needs to keep his head down and appreciate Frankenstein for giving him an escape hatch out of the menace of civil rule. But, Igor also knows he knows what Frankenstein doesn't know.

Igor isn't an example of a man of books and studied know-how. That guy is the scientist Dr. Frankenstein.

Igor is an agent of making do and invention on the fly. Working with what's at hand. Digging in the dark by the light of the moon. Harvesting and transporting viable body parts in a basket filled with carrots. Avoiding detection as he moves through the crowd assembled in the public square and calling for his death.

Igor goes on hunch and inspiration. Assembling veins and arteries and nerve webs and ducts and muscles and all the assorted orders of tubes running the endless inner channels of the body have taught him this. How to make do. How to work within systems beyond comprehension. He adapts a left foot for a right, perhaps, and learns something unfathomable. He fashions a vagina from some ears, and the body reveals some impossible secret.

Igor attracts the lightening of chance that is necessary to activate the brutal blossom of desire—that urge enabling us to defy death after the finish of every breath.

So, yeah, an Igor would be helpful to have on hand when changing from one skin into another.

But, I don't have one. I have to make do alone.

Wow. What a digression. Sorry about that.

16

Anyway, back to my point. I started telling you about getting skinned.

Having a willing assistant would be very helpful, and an Igor would be great. But, realistically, given the nature of the job, putting on a skin often becomes a solitary activity.

While hospitals are stocked with surgeons and nurses who are experts in anatomy, they usually hesitate when things start to edge into the illicit. Sometimes I can find a surgery nurse or paramedic who for one reason or another does freelance work, but they are not always so reliable. I'm not some storybook vampire with unlimited funds and freelancer medics usually are able to get more money from working underground fighting events.

I used to think that morticians would be good people to befriend and get help from, but I found them more skilled in cosmetic practices. Undertakers are not so able to deal with the structural intricacies of putting on a skin. They prefer things to be static and permanently attached in place. The morticians I talked with also seemed to harbor some conflicting interests about letting the skins of dead people keep roaming the world.

To be fair, morticians have to suffer their own societal stigmas, so I can't blame them for their caution.

Taxidermists, on the other hand, are a promising area that I am yet to explore. They might be a good fit.

Of course, putting on a skin is just one side of the practice. Skins have to be taken off, too.

Removing a skin involves its own very delicate aspects. But, gravity makes removal much simpler and once you've learned the basic things to be cautious about, it is not so difficult to take off a skin alone. For example, I recommend that you take special care to leave the feet and hands turned inside-out when taking off a skin. This does three useful things:

First, it helps to air-out places where a fair amount of bodily juices settle. The hands and feet are places which are usually below other stuff—at the ends of extremities—and thus they are where gravity naturally brings odd liquids to settle.

Second, it is easier to put the hands and feet of a skin back on by rolling the skin back across these complexly jointed bone structures. Trying to slide the sinew and muscle enwrapped bones of toes and fingers down inside the narrow, delicate and rather adhesive tubes of a skin's hands and feet is tough work. Making adjustments to the position and tension is easier if the skeletal structures are already in position at the tips and you can push from within. If you don't do this, the process demands too much tugging from the outside or at the forearms and calves, causing unsightly scratches or possibly weird stretch marks that can make people who you might meet later imagine you suffered some injury or just make them just feel uncomfortable.

Mitigating suspicions always makes life easier in this world.

Third, leaving the hands and feet turned inside-out is a good way to hide the fact that the odd object piled in your closet is a human skin. Should someone be in your house and by accident see a skin you have, usually they can't tell what it is if it is not right-side-out. Efforts to camouflage the skin as a blanket or semi-collapsed leather tote bag are usually ruined if an overly curious house guest spots fingernails or toenails.

Care in storage is important.

17

The relative ease of removing a skin is very different from trying to put one on, especially alone. The main reason for the difficulty is the pure weight of a human skin.

The skin is the largest organ of the body. While a skin might feel like nothing when it is evenly distributed, correctly fitted across the skeleton and the muscles are filling it out, things change when it's a mass to move around on its own. When a skin is folded or collapsed inside a storage box, or just spread out on a floor, it's heavy and cumbersome. Its weight makes it impossible to simply lift it up and climb inside.

A skin isn't some sort of leather jump-suit.

As well, picking a skin up from any particular spot—such as by the shoulders—causes a lot of stress on the sections that hang down. The skin can stretch in weird ways or it can even tear.

Definitely not good.

If you have an assistant, he or she can help the process by kind of pouring the skin over you. This allows gravity to help. But an assistant can also help control the flow of how much skin I have to deal with as the process proceeds.

Usually, pouring on a skin is done after first laying it onto a large board. Then the board is propped up in a way so that I can position myself lower than the board's edge. After that, the board is tilted and the skin kind of flows off as I get inside it.

First, I roll on the feet. Then, I roll on the hands. Then, the assistant tilts the board and gravity lets the rest of the skin flow into place across my burrowing body.

But, like I said, usually having help isn't an option.

If I am putting on a skin alone, I usually have to lay the skin on the floor. I put on the feet and hands first and then kind of slither into the rest of it. I slowly move the skin over me in a way that probably looks like it is absorbing me into itself.

I start seated on the floor, but once the feet and hands are in place, I lay on my side with the skin kind of halfway inside-out. I move into it from that angle. Once I'm inside, I seal the back closed and try to sit up.

When a skin is first put on it is still pretty loose across the muscles, so sitting up can be challenging. Lots of slippage can occur, all of which needs to be adjusted later. I like to have a rope hanging near by to help me pull myself up to a standing position.

In either process—with help or alone—the face is left to last.

And if the skin fits well enough (as opposed to how tight André Cadere's face fits), it is quite easy to slide the face over the skull and adjust it into place.

The skull is the biggest lump of bone and not as soft and sticky as other more muscled areas. This makes it easier to slide the face into place. As well, there is an enthusiasm that comes from knowing this difficult and time-consuming process is almost complete.

Adrenaline is a very valuable assistant.

It can take about 3 hours to put on a skin by myself. With assistance, maybe about 1 hour. Removal takes about 20 to 30 minutes. Packing a skin and hiding it away, another 15 to 20.

Don't rush any of the steps or you'll be sorry.

18

Crossroads once served our psychospatial purposes of being not quite one place or another.

Doubled zones.

As bisecting oppositions, crossroads attracted conflicted spirits.

One line to a distance as equally empty as the other three. As open. As nowhere or as promising of somewhere. As elsewhere. As where you need to go. As equally potent and portending.

Crossroads used to be layered with turbulences. The flow from and to four destinations rippled through each other, causing a boil of agitated differences.

Crossed goals.

Misdirections.

A chaos.

And so, crossroads were the place to go to meet the devil, to contact that which isn't natural or aligned with the directional logics of cause and effect. Not of from and to. Not of here and there.

Contrarians and double-dealers.

Soul snatchers.

Magic makers.

If you wanted to have unearned powers, go to the crossroads.

If you wanted what no one else humanly deserved—immortality or another's lover—go to the crossroads.

At the crossroads, the impossible could be asserted and snared.

At the crossroads, you could turn the world to your wish.

At the crossroads you could find chances against the odds.

You. Could. Fuck. The. Odds.

But, no more.

That was the past.

Now, traffic lights have usurped the devil's powers.

Now, crossroads are constantly monitored and directed. By machine logics. By rules. By authority.

Hyper-regulated, futures are predictably programmed. Directions are given to determined destinations, and their distances, and the weather you'll find on the way.

Time has become sequenced. Red light. Green light. Yellow light. Red light. Green light. Yellow light. Every moment is dictated and enforced. Measured with starts and ends.

Robot traffic cops finger their data ticket books. Cameras scan license plates and facial biometrics. Before you even get to the next light, a fine has been printed and sent towards your house. It's there before you are.

They know where to find you. You have a residence and it's linked to the pattern stored in the distances between your eyes, nostrils, cheekbones, mouth and jowls.

Your face is your address.

You are identified before you even know you decided to run the light. You are punished before you even feel the desire to exceed your limit.

This crossroads of selves is being regulated.

And, thus, now drivers obey the law. They learn to never approach excesses of self. They learn there is no way around it. No way to slip between gaps. Gaps are new forms of traps.

Be. Suspicious. Of. Yourself.

What were once the crossroads' chaos of excess and turbulent overflow have now been replaced with a constantly topped-off accuracy, leaving no space for either more-than-enough or a vacuum.

Now, the crossroads are officiated. It's either exclusively this way or exclusively that. No confusion allowed. One way after one way. When one direction is on, the other is off. Go or stop.

God now holds the crossing flows apart.

No demonic outside chance.

Wait your turn.

The deity of laws restricts overabundance and potential. There is an order for this way or that.

19

Nearing the location for the drug festival, I couldn't see or hear anything too much out of the ordinary. Turn-out for the event was dying off more and more each year.

I turned the corner from Midosuji onto Doshoumachi.

I walked towards the shrine and noticed a few clusters of participants. Not much density, but still worth calling a crowd. I took a spot between two hunched-over and very elderly ladies near a red curbside mail box.

One lady had a wheeled walker. It had a faded flowered seat so she could sit down whenever necessary. Her little machine of emergent properties was wrought with super-powers enabling her to be more than she could be on her own.

Humanity equals tool use.

She had tied a large number of plastic bags to her rolling chair, so it looked something like a dirty little poly-vinyl cloud. She was sitting in her cloud when I came up.

With her hands wedged firmly against her knees, she propped up her upper body and stared into the street. Obviously, she was saving her energy for dashing out and fighting for drugs. I could see her strategy very clearly. She'd push out from the curb and use the walker to block others in the hunt. She'd use her frailty and age to establish a territory. Then, she'd open the seat and stow drugs inside the compartment under that lid. It was a good plan. I decided to give her her space. I didn't want to get tripped up or entangled by her machinery. She was an intelligent and strategic threat that deserved respect. A machine of wisdom.

The other woman was wearing a lumpy white surgical mask, but seemed less prepared than Ms. Rolling Chair for grabbing drugs. She merely had an old plastic bag that she obviously planned to use to store medicines. A poorly prepared plan, but that was my plan too.

I'd brought a plastic bag, also. But, mine was newer. As well, my plan was to try and get a variety of drugs.

These ladies were surely just after distinct pain killers. They looked like they were kind of under the influence of something already. Their gazes were overly focused and they barely talked to each other. Just the occasional mention of the obvious, like, "It'll start soon." Or, "I wish they'd start." Or, "My legs hurt. I hope I get some joint cream."

This was a common topic shared between gatherers. Everybody made it known what their main drug goal was. This served two purposes: a) to learn who to move away from in order to avoid conflicts due to shared desires. And b) to know who to go to if you wanted to trade something. It saved a lot of time afterwards.

The efficiencies of conflicting hopes.

And so, the parade-goers looked at me with an odd confusion when I said I was happy to get anything.

"Even lady drugs?" one old man in an overly stretched knit cap joked.

"Sure. I'll try them," I said, half-way looking to see how he'd react.

He just moved across the street without comment.

As 10am approached, I could hear things getting ready inside the shrine. There was a ceremony being done to formally thank the pair of gods in charge of bringing prosperity to the medicine industry. Some *sake* was poured and offered. Some sacred objects were shook. A horn made of a large shell was blown by an ascetic employed by the shrine for such rites. As well, a big kettle-like bell was rattled.

Then, after what felt like a long time, the first float moved out onto the street and turned right. We all cheered inside, but outwardly we just watched for the right moment to make our move.

The old lady with the rolling chair stood up and got ready to push off. She looked like a frightened astronaut about to depart in a damaged pod.

This year's theme was The Zoo of Healing, commemorating the menagerie of beasts that have played a part in the history of medicinal R&D.

The first float exiting the shrine was of a large tiger. I'd seen it before. It was somewhat abstract, as tigers go. But obviously a tiger. The black and yellow stripes made sure of that. At certain angles, it was more realistic than at other angles. Its claws were reaching out in an exaggerated way, as though a tiger's claws are the main purpose of a tiger's being. As though a tiger's main identifying quality is its claws.

I'd never thought about that. For me, a tiger has always been about the stripes. Of course, the fangs and claws are important, but not particularly unique. I really couldn't tell a tiger's claws from a lion's or a bear's. A tiger is about the stripes for me.

But, this float was obviously emphasizing the claws. Or, it was simply a design mistake. Or a production mistake.

Anyway, the tiger came out first and was followed by the slow-moving procession of other animals. A boar. A rooster. Another rooster. A flexible shark, moving as though swimming in a zig-zag flow from side to side across the street. A rhino. A whole bunch of slightly larger than life-sized turtles. Another rooster. A rippling river of maybe 25 snakes. A massive armadillo, its scaly armor layered and detailed with bits of blue. A lizard. And then something I couldn't make any sense of. It looked like a huge fist raised in protest at a labor march.

I asked the old woman next to me and she said it was a panther paw.

Just a paw?

When I asked why, she ignored me and focused on getting her gathering face on.

As the line of animals approached, I could see them more clearly. Many of them were made of artistically molded plastic and colorful foil. The same materials that are used to make pill packaging and drug capsules were used to make the bodies of the beasts. The skins of these creatures were more stylistically colored than realistic, and many were translucent to allow us to see inside.

And within the skins' surfaces, illuminated images were created by dimly shifting lights. These projections showed the animals' internal organs and bodily functions in action. Blood circulating. Lungs inflating. Hair growing. Muscles flexing. Glands pumping out currents of fluid, etc.

Along with these internal functions, other internal projections also showed what human affliction was healed by that particular area of the animal's body. Human lungs inflated and deflated in animated repetition across the inside of a see-through lizard's tale. A human brain pulsed in pain in the eyes of a tortoise. Inside of a rabbit, a pair of human female ovaries released a shining golden egg into a uterus, which then swelled against the growth of a curled fetus. Male human heads swelling full of dark hair appeared on the skins of snakes. Erect penises glowed like glimmering city skylines within the bodies of the roosters. A sneezing nose stopped mid-eruption in the shark's brain.

There was too much to take in, and I reminded myself that I had a job to do.

First things first, André. Get ready for drug time!

And no sooner than I caught myself thinking too much did the key moment arrive.

The floats moved along the street like a vague caravan of ghosts, but not of their own accord. Each animal was held aloft by a stick. And each stick was held aloft by a child, dressed in what I thought were clown outfits.

I couldn't figure out any reason why the children should be dressed as clowns, except simply because this was a festival and clowns are always festive. But I was mistaken. I was later told that in fact the children were costumed in white smocks, like laboratory workers and druggists. It was just the odd use of excessive white-face make-up and red lipstick which made them look like clowns to me.

Anyway, as the children paraded down the street, they would stop on cue and begin to violently shake the animal that they were keeping in the air. In these spasms of thrash, small yellow-and-black-striped rectangles would fall out of the animals' bodies and come clattering down onto the street.

These were the drug packs that we were all waiting for.

Each box was filled with whatever left-over drugs got placed inside. There was no labeling on the striped boxes. Just the tiger stripes.

This was the random rain I had hoped for.

The boxes made a beautiful, softly percussive sound when they hit the ground.

And, thus, the gatherers began to slowly rush into the street. Not wanting to appear overly eager at first, the general energy was of casually crossing the street en masse. And, mostly, gatherers gave each other space. It was surprisingly genteel this year. While on occasion a few gatherers would be intent on the same group of tiger rectangles and a dash followed by a scramble would erupt, these usually ended in laughter at the shared absurdity of what everyone was doing.

Regardless, the people gathered all the drugs from the street and stored them in bags, backpacks, pockets or beneath walker seats. There were smiles all around and a few brief flashes of competitive thrust.

That's what festivals are for, right?

All told, I got 26 boxes, filled with a mix of sleeping pills, diarrhea medicine, hemorrhoid cream, cold tablets, menstrual pain pills, cough drops and a bunch of fever capsules. An elderly woman wanted to trade some headache medicine for my menstrual pills to give to her daughter, but I refused. I wanted to try it. I traded the hemorrhoid cream to an old man for some kind of inhalable powder that does something for itching. I couldn't understand from the instructions what it did. My favorite kind of medicine. I might mix it with something else and go crazy.

One middle-aged woman in a tight purple sweater came up to me and touched my arm. She looked at my face and gently tapped the Cadere-inspired stick I was carrying. I think she thought I must be blind and she gave me some eye drops without asking for anything in exchange. Nice score for random cocktail ingredients. Thanks.

As we finished trading drugs and admiring what each other were lucky enough to gather, the parade continued on down Doshoumachi.

I decided to follow the parade off the back and collect any missed tiger boxes. But nothing survived the other gatherers down the route.

As I walked behind the parade, I emptied out the contents of my various tiger boxes from my plastic collection bag and into the big blue shoulder bag I was carrying. I slung its strap over the back of my neck. Wearing the bag like a huge bib, I poured the drugs into its open space. So many shiny colors rained in and mixed together. Their plastic and foil wrappers whispered a special static-derived song as I rummaged through them. I compressed all the empty tiger boxes and stored them in one of the blue bag's pockets. Then, I roughly sorted through the jumble of drug packages. Capsules, pills, liquids, powders, gels, inhalants and smokes.

I found a shimmering purple foil-backed strip of yellow tablets that seemed to be for some sort of inner-ear infection. I popped one out of its carapace and held it between my fingers. I said to it, "You are the first" and raised it toward the sky like a tiny sun.

Oddly, I lost sight of the tiny yellow pill as I passed a building that had one wall painted exactly the same color.

As my fingers moved the pill upward and my eyes followed it, my vision lost track of it in the context of the yellow background wall. I felt a sudden panic of absence and loss. Some immediate lack or existential theft.

My paranoia-brain flashed brightly, shouting that the pill had been snatched from my grip or that I had stupidly somehow dropped it by carelessness. Immediately after, my sceptic's-brain doubted that it had ever even been in my hand from the get-go. How did I really know I had a hold of it after I removed it from its package? Could I really trust my sense of touch?

My fingers could still feel it, but my eyes could not confirm it out there at arm's reach. This dissonance required a test for truth. So, my fingers squeezed harder to double-prove the pill's dense existence. Of course, the pill had to respond as well, so the sunny little yellow tablet shot out against the pressure and bounced across the blacktop.

Click click click.

I lunged to catch it, but it scuttled off like a white rabbit down a storm drain.

"Shit!"

But, not to worry, my concerned reader. There were more pills where that one came from. So I just popped out another yellow dot and swallowed it without any special ceremony.

Soon after passing the pill-yellow wall, I came to the end of Doshoumachi Street. I turned left where the parade of floats carried by clownly-painted children turned right.

I paused, turned around and watched them vanish. I could hear the fading sound of the parade almost too clearly.

Then, I held up my colorfully striped stick and waved it in the air, as though I was magically blessing the parade's conclusion.

20

It could be argued that the stick is the oldest human tool.

Imagine its versatility: to span and support, to be thrown and swung, to roll and wedge and pry and scratch. To poke. To block. To whack. To impale. To make a whirring sound when swung through the air.

While some people might point at the rock as the first tool, the stick gets my vote.

The stick is also just so damned dramatic. A rock is maybe good for keeping secretly hidden in a hand behind your back and then bluntly crushing the skull of an unsuspecting enemy or a god-damned trusting dimwit. But nobody uses a rock for much now.

The stick still has a visual flair and has endured much longer than the rock.

A stick is charismatic and has a "look at me" power. It is perfect for being seen and contemplated from afar. It inspires wonder and questions. Caution and fear. How far can it fly? Witnesses pause and assess, their minds churning out vague potential futures that the stick could bring about. A stick can reach out and crack a collarbone or puncture a gut. It can get a hat from a tree or test the depth of a lake. It can be climbed to reach a peach or to escape from a freak. Bundled together, sticks increase in strength. They can block an attack or block the wind, hold up a roof, cage a danger, protect a treasure.

A stick can kill and you don't get no blood on you.

Nobody doesn't notice the person wielding a stick. It can be dramatically sunk into mud and remain standing, like it has a will and purpose all its own. Like it has its own desire.

A stick is always used for commanding magic because it naturally directs attention, or can misdirect. A stick seems to have an independence of intention. Like it is endowed with something beyond a tool.

The stick is maybe the first philosophical machine. It hums with concept and transcendence. It is metaphysical. It points and extends beyond. The stick inspires—everything from pointers, walls, wands, swords, spears and spires.

If it were honest, the field of architecture would surely list the stick as its genesis.

Want to raise a flag? Get a stick.

In this way, sticks maintain an intoxicating potency even all these eons after the first one was lifted out of a tangle of forest breakage and used to help in digging a hole, or walking with an injury, or beating the life from an attacker or abandoned infant.

A stick that is carried in public without an obvious purpose is still met with puzzled, awe-struck or terrorized looks. Carried by a person, a stick that is free of intentions—not having an easily identifiable use—orients the space of minds around it.

Carrying one of his sticks, Cadere would attend gallery opening events thrown for other artists. He would walk about the gallery space looking at the works, mingle, drink and chat. Always with the stick. He'd casually be in the space of the other with his own artwork.

With a stick, he'd intrude. Invade. Pollute. Deflate.

And true to the motto, "If there isn't a picture, it doesn't exist," Cadere would get photos taken of his sticks' presence at the shows he attended. Proof of his invasions and occupations of rival territory.

At times, a picture would feature his stick standing alone in the corner of a famous gallery director's office. The seat of power.

Other photos show his sticks propped up next to gallery entrances. Sometimes, a stick would be documented leaning against a gallery wall with the featured artwork being exhibited mutely in the background, as if the authorized art works were crying: "Everybody is only supposed to look at ME."

In every photo, Cadre's stick held the space, orienting those rarified and exclusionary worlds around itself. The stick became a disputed center of attention. The stick inserted itself and established a conditionality of the space which sapped the gallery of its determined and purchased authority.

The stick undermined assuredness.

The stick questioned.

The stick stood in for Cadere, even in his absence.

Like the rumor of a secret loose in a room, Cadere's sticks had their own gravitational power and drew attention towards themselves. Sometimes this was a welcome challenge that played against exhausting art-world norms. Other times his sticks were viewed as a rude ploy to parasitically suck attention away from the authorized artworks that were attached to the gallery's exclusive and expensive walls.

The sticks served both these but also other ends. Like levers prying open the seams of power, Cadere's sticks critically exposed how space is controlled by the gallery system, and thereby how the flows of interaction between artists, viewers and buyers are controlled by owners and other agents in power.

This was Cadere's real artwork, to destabilize such political dynamics. To drive a stake into the heart of the space. To tear into the body of art and access its secrets.

His sticks served the purpose of splitting power open for the picking. For redispersal and autopsification.

21

Maybe from having seen too many ghostly floating exotic animals, my eyes were having some difficulty focusing. Or maybe it was from popping a couple more mystery pills from a shiny gold package with the graphic of a glowing blue molecule on the front. Anyway, for whatever reason, things were going sort-of fuzzy and buzzy at their edges. The world was going gooey. People were blurblurring, glazing like smears of color eroding to fade. Walkers were melting in their flow. Even the trustworthy vertical lines of buildings were reverbing along themselves too much, into triplicate, quadruplicate, quintuplicate.

Echocococo.

My eyes felt bloaty and overpacked as well. Swollen and pressurized.

It crossed my mind that maybe I was losing my eyesight. Maybe the middle-aged woman in the purple sweater who'd assumed my stick was for blindness had been right. Also, I had lost the pill in the color of the wall. How did that happen? Was I going blind and was the stick I was carrying an unconscious foreshadow of that infirmary rather than my intended allusion to Cadere?

How to know the real causes of effects?

Terminalia is about observing ends and maybe going beyond them. So, my thoughts raced and I fretted that maybe one of the limits I was going to exceed on that day was to go beyond the visual threshold and into the world of the sightless.

My mind went stumbling and tumbling over that fear.

Were the random choices I'd made really signs and portending hints of a destined stint in visual darkness? I felt my body trying to exert sweat. My meat was fighting to release the pressure of that fear. But Cadere's skin didn't oblige. The gap between those worlds—between the he and the me—would not meet and so my paranoia just bubbled within.

And maybe the blindness was conditional. Maybe Cadere's skin was the cause. Maybe his skin was the thing to blame. Did he go blind while alive? Did he have some disease about vision that I didn't know about?

I didn't know.

I never read anything about that.

But maybe he didn't know about it when he was alive either. He died of cancer at 44, so maybe his blindness was still to come. Was his skin contaminated with a genetic timeline he never lived long enough to activate, but now I was living it? Was what wasn't his future now becoming mine?

Had I bought a dormant vessel of death?

What a rip-off!

I felt trapped in a thick, heavy sack of betrayal.

For a few minutes, anyway.

Then my mind found some logical work-arounds.

Perhaps his skin was just constricting the bone structure around my eyes enough to make me kind of seem to be going blind? Perhaps the relative smallness of his face was simply pinching my eye-balls. Cadere's skin obviously included his eyelids, so maybe those were putting too much pressure on my eye-balls and warping my vision.

That all seemed more logical and less permanent. The skin wasn't betraying me. It would stretch. It was just changing the way I saw, warping sight, making shapes go out of shape and affecting the clarity of edges, making things become other things.

The skin was producing unknowns.

But why just now? Why not earlier or last week? What was special with today?

Anyway, with this new reasoning, I felt less panic. I could put my more serious fears of blindness to rest a bit.

My vision was just being tweaked, maybe. I wasn't really going blind, probably.

Or, I wasn't going really blind blind. Conditionally blind, perhaps. Maybe a temporary thing.

This reassurance of safety—born from the bent logic I'd just fabricated—allowed me to more playfully imagine pretending to go blind.

Without the fear of really going blind, I could imagine negative outcomes in a creative way. When there is no real worry, I can more safely amp up the terror potential and speculate a graphic—if fantastic—tragedy. For fun sake.

My personal epic drama.

I then considered, what would it be like to go blind? Temporarily totally blind.

It became a thought-experiment in blindness.

I thought that the situation I was in on the street was kind of an interesting chance to try blindness out, to take it for a test drive by walking around the city in a new-found state of profound lostness. What would it be like to walk the streets without sight, to guess at edges and leap into the abyss from curbs? The notion felt thrilling and seemed without much real risk. A bit of disability tourism. A little bit of cultural appropriation without the seriously life-altering side-effects of permanent blindness.

Vicarious handicapping.

I thought about it for a moment and quickly I realized that aside from sleep there are really no more than very brief flashes of sightlessness in my life. Vision fills every detail of the frame I view through.

I blink and don't really seem to miss anything.

Of course, I'm completely dismissing the vast and constant unseen beyond my peripheral vision. What's behind me? And what is beyond the color spectrum? What's microscopic?

Out of sight, out of mind.

Such ignorances don't worry me because the degree of vision I have gives me the sense that I'm seeing everything. Vision makes me confident that everything I can see is all that there is to see.

Is that confidence?

More likely, it's cockiness, because what better definition of a small-minded ignoramus could we come up with than someone who thinks that what he can see is all there is to see? Only when we can imagine that there are perspectives beyond our own can we get a hint for the vastness we are merely a part of. When we can fathom that there are visions other than ours—that there are ways to see the world from within someone else's skin—only then can we get a context and scale for our own limited movement through the world.

Wow, that all sounds sermonesque, doesn't it?

Put another way, limiting what is possible to think to only what I think—or can think—is just so fucking boring.

So, I started to consider what it could be like to be blind, to walk around blind and rely on my other senses. At least for a while. How would this city that feels so familiar to me feel if I moved through even a couple hundred meters of it in an up-close, first-hand and absolute darkness? What would life feel like within a temporarily blind man's skin?

So, as I was walking in Osaka with my colorful stick in hand, I committed myself to a total blindness.

I closed my eyes.

22

Immediately, my body froze. With the sense I'd learned to rely on as my main one gone, my body let sirens of caution instantly scream. As natural and spontaneous as a reflex, my sense of touch desired to reach out for some measure of surenesses. My senses scrambled for information.

My (or rather André's) feet and skin became a million distinct centers of knowing, probing out beyond the edge of me for risk/benefit assessments. The skin flashed alive in ways that the eyes' authority had been keeping dormant.

The textures of the street flooded up to me with potential threats to consider or lines of direction to trust. Every pebble and crack whispered that a possible danger was looming: a curb or a ditch or a pile of sharp trash.

What can the nape of the neck read of threat? What can the hair detect?

I moved the stick in front of my feet, letting it check for what it could, for dangers conveyed through sudden vertical surfaces or changes in the stick's tapping sound.

The flow of the stick smoothly sliding without any glitch reassured me that forward motion was okay. The lack of contact became the sense of proceeding. A feeling I'd never really had before. It was the moment to moment, location to location, flow of going blind. To sense no blockage felt like pure speed, even for just a few meters.

Into the void. The energy of proceeding.

But the suddenness with which changes could appear made me careful to not predict much beyond the next footstep. The abrupt catch of the stick would stop me totally, reassert a lostness that wasn't simply searching for other choices, but was rather a dizzying disorientation within minor angles. The unknown was flush with dangers that were too numerous to list.

Caution's siren would sing and sing.

A profound paranoia.

Imagining that just to the left of my head might be a protruding pole but just to the right could be a looming truck mirror created a vivid saturation of torments. An ankle-twisting pothole could be a moment away. A fallen bicycle. A low-hanging electric wire. Time and space became packed with secret attackers. But likewise, the millimeters of miss became equal to meters or miles. If I missed hitting a shop sign by a centimeter, it was equal to its complete non-existence.

Out of sight might be out of mind, but the untouched doesn't even exist.

I'd usually thought that being lost meant to scan a mysterious visual landscape and not find any familiar landmark. Lostness was a 360-degree pan of unrecognizable buildings, signage and no known direction towards any relocating anchor.

But the lostness of blindness was a radical body intimacy with unknown immediacies.

In blindness, my body is always lost within the relative distances between me and potential impalements or the stealthy appearances of objects that might trip me up. As I walked blind down a street, an open truck door or a tree branch or a person's lazy umbrella were always already available threats.

My imagination flooded my mind with paranoia juice. My body was an exposed target of too many potential aiming trajectories to reasonably fathom. But, these trajectories were not coming at me. I was lostly seeking them. I was subjecting myself onto them. I was the one to blame.

If I was stabbed in the cheek or throat or ribs or thigh or groin or knee or ankle, each was a different alignment of me inflicting the wound upon myself. I'd walk into the silent motorcycle handlebar. I'd put out my eyeball on the barber pole's point. I'd actively move into trajectories of collision that exist on a schedule of presences. I'd time my demise but be dumb to it. Because, if my right foot is present in the place at the time that a bucket is present in the place, I will kick it. Death is partly about enacting that conditional embrace with ignorance.

But, the salvation of it all is the porousness of being, the abundance of relative gaps. If my foot misses the bucket by just a millimeter, it might as well be a mile, or a thousand, or 10,000. The bucket's silence makes it nowhere. If my eyebrow doesn't hit the corner of a protruding ramen shop sign, I might as well be wrapped in a protective cloud of angel bubbles.

"There but for the grace of God go I. There with the grace of God go I."

Being lost is to not recognize my surroundings, to see myself saturated in differences. But to be blind is to not have the luxury of time that distances give.

To move in the world blind is to both wear my difference close to the skin and also to recognize my surroundings as my skin. My skin becomes known via the world's exotic and familiar qualities. In blindness, I am the world of differences. Thus, lostness can be felt tingling across the body's innumerable points as they search for differences. To be blind is to become the differences that give hints for locating myself in place.

The skin is always already feeling something, and the most important feeling is nothing.

From the feeling of nothing, the skin gets the quickest hints of where a difference occurs. From a base of nothing, I can potentially notice the location and aspects of a difference quickly enough to adjust my distance and angle before the corner of a wooden planter box digs into the pain layers of my knee.

Walking blind, my skin and hair and hearing and sense of smell were always gathering moments and directions of sense experiences that vision usually has me just abandon because my eyes offer such ease about distances. In blindness, this abandoned abundance becomes viscerally evident. In blindness, the ever-assembling traces of the body's swim through lostness are ever-present.

But, I had to stop being blind.

I couldn't keep my blindness going for more than maybe 50 meters without opening my eyes and letting vision take back control.

Vision immediately gave me the sense of predictability, of knowing at the speed of light what was up ahead or coming my way.

The intimacy of lostness immediately became merely a surface resting at a safe distance, not the hulking intimacy of fear scenting my every inhalation and buzzing like an aura of threats over my skin.

23

Having abandoned my eyes-closed blindness experiment, I wondered more about the social. How might other people react to seeing me blind?

I don't mean about how people who I know might react in emotional surprise and emotional empathy if they learned I'd lost my sight. Rather, I wondered about how random strangers I would pass on the streets might react to seeing a blind person in general. Would I be able to sense a difference in the way people act towards me if they think I'm blind? Could I see something that I am currently blind to because I can see?

I decided to give it a try. Even though the colorful stick I was carrying wasn't the typical white cane of the blind, its thinness and length looked right enough to at least make some people automatically read me as blind. The purple-sweatered woman thought so.

But, how should I act if I was blind? How should I perform blindness? Should I tap the stick? Should I close my eyes? Should I make my eyes wander wildly and confused? Should I buy some black sunglasses to really sell the idea with some costuming? I opted for doing a bit of tapping, but mainly to just let the stick search the space in front of my feet as though it were serving as a cautious antenna. And I didn't want to close my eyes. Instead, I decided to let my focus go vague. I'd keep my eyes open, but not look at anything in particular. I'd not follow anything with vision.

I mentally categorized my level of pretend blindness to be not complete blindness. For me, my level of blindness was one that allowed me to see vague shapes but not really make things out very clearly. So, in my blindness, I knew where large objects were—such as buildings and cars and nearby people—but I couldn't see detail well at all. That was the danger for me.

I was not severely blind. I was sincerely blind.

And, because I wasn't really blind at all, I could observe people in their reactions because my eyes would be open.

So, I gave it a try for a little while.

In general, the people I saw fell into four categories: 1) those who simply didn't notice me at all, 2) those who noticed me but didn't show any reaction, 3) those who reacted with caution and actively got out of the way of the path that my stick indicated I was moving into, 4) and those who just seemed more interested by the stick itself without ever considering it to be a blind person's cane. The last group just stared at the stick as we passed each other.

I pretended to be blind for about three blocks but I stopped it when I saw a building slowly collapse and vanish into an empty lot. That had an undeniable drama that made me quickly abandon my social experiment regarding blindness.

And, while the self-deconstructing building could have been a side effect of mixing together the blue molecules and the wall-colored pill with an itch powder which I swallowed between opening my eyes and starting my social experiment, the experience of watching the building go gone was so vivid, engrossing and dazzling that I was drawn to it like a newly realized desire.

I stood there watching it for the whole time it lasted.

24

As though it was a dream, the four-story building vibrated and shivered behind a chin-high fence of black iron bars. The fence's vertical bars remained completely static, which made the building's shaking even more evident in contrast.

The building's lines became blurry, as though everything making it was shimmering against itself. Isolated from the surrounding calm, the building looked like it was experiencing a private and self-localized earthquake, something catastrophic but reserved for only its particular plot of land and interiors. A self-quake rumbling throughout each of the building's various structural centers. All its heres and theres were in extreme agitation.

As the shaking went on, I expected the building to start shedding pieces, fall apart and then crash down into a violent pile of dusty rubble. But it didn't. The building just gradually faded away. Over the time I watched it, its particles of form gradually drifted off from their shared stability. From an office building to building blocks to bits of blocks to dust motes to a cloudy churn to nothing.

Throughout it all, the iron bars remained perfectly still. Even when I walked up and touched them, the bars contained no vibration. But, behind them, the building violently rattled and dramatically departed from being itself.

I reached my hand through the black bars. In that beyond, I could feel the energy from the rattling space. I couldn't touch the building itself, but the energy of its transformation beat the air like a massive motor.

But, totally silent.

There was no volume to the destruction at all.

The building's shaking seemed to be happening at the same rate everywhere throughout its form, but limited to just its piece of Osaka property.

The building was evenly losing itself throughout itself, everywhere at once. Rather than one isolated section becoming weaker than the rest and then collapsing under the pressure from the stronger sections, this building was just coming apart bit beside bit. Surface by surface, connection by connection and form by form, the building was becoming undone.

As the violence progressed, I could see through the building's structures—through the reddish-brown ceramic tiles and the reinforced concrete walls that the tiles encased, but also through all the furniture, fixtures, flooring and stuff of functions that were inside. As though the density of a fog were dissolving into a haze and then gradually into a clarity, the plot of land became empty of the building and everything it contained.

All of it vanished, leaving no trace or even any mark in the dirt. All was gone, except for a white plastic mailbox that was wired to a wooden post just outside the building's property.

The ground was covered with a fine, grey powder, not dissimilar to the itch medicine I'd taken earlier.

I walked over to the mailbox and could see that it was packed full of stuff.

I opened its unlocked door and pieces of paper attempted to pour out.

I held back the postal cascade with my hand. The box was stuffed with take-out food fliers, roof repair ads, discount-day coupons at an adult video shop and other junk mail. Numerous pieces of real mail were also tightly overpacked into the box.

I felt in a daze from the building's performance, but a strong burst of déjà-vu urged me to take one package out of the rest.

To just steal it.

Not motivated by any sense of want, it was just pure theft. I felt no sense of doing wrong. Just a clean urge to take for taking's sake.

It was a thick beige envelope with a stain on a corner.

I sensed this was kind of a precious document.

The sender was something called Famularo Industries.

25

A desire path is an unauthorized trail that inserts a marginal assertion into a programmed declaration of what is and isn't, should be and shouldn't.

A desire path is unmade. It skirts the bounds of public discourse. It walks on the wild side.

A desire path reveals the anarchic trajectory available within every regulated angle and each measured design of movement. It flows against the spirit of the compositional. It cuts a softness right across the hard and fast.

Arising from no one traveler alone, a desire path claims a space without dictate or orchestration. It lays plans to waste. It glows as practice, and then vanishes once the pattern of movement decays.

It exists as pure use.

If a factory closes, its desire paths vanish. Its backdoor entrance gets fenced off. The guard dogs are rounded up, sold or put down. Weeds erase all trace.

Unattached to any time or bigger purpose, a desire path runs short cuts between forevers and infects the determined gods of planning with a mortal trace.

A desire path breathes with life and activity and passage and need.

It may be a dirt track worn into place where pedestrians cut a corner off a section of pavement that was designed by landscape planners to bring imagined strollers from here to there, but around that way.

A desire path softens off the right angles.

A desire path gives permission.

A desire path stands as evidence of a gathered and collective flow. It shows where people or creatures or maybe even materials follow a movement that is counter to a certainty assumed by designed intentions.

It's the crow's flight.

It's the wise man's method to "appear like magic" rather than "make an entrance."

A desire path hacks the systemic grandeur and ruled processes toward destinations. Instead, it enshrines a nod to those who are in the know. It shines as a measure of unregistered resistance.

It is erosional and under-determinable.

In the mind, desire paths also appear.

When learned patterns are left to ossify and go quiet through the instincts of know-how and the new, then desire-path modes of completing thoughts arise as bits of improvised flair.

Perhaps it's a self-wrought logic, or the thread of an unnamed sense that is followed often enough to make the course of the thought's pattern become deeply one's own. Ingrained knowledge. A personal rote method. At least for as long as that path of short-cut-thinking serves.

It's an instinct for dealing with familiar situations. A cut to the chase.

At times it's useful and time-saving. At other times, it's just lazy.

A desire path of thought can be an unchallenged prejudice fulfilling some secretly held hope, expectation or fucked-up rationalization.

It can be a particular bent-logic for why cats are helping to heal you. Some privately duct-taped heuristic that justifies holding a grudge or keeping a lucky number. It can be a conspiracy of cherry-picked bullshit that falls apart if you try to explain it to someone else, but your mind knows the secret-danger dance-moves to get you that squirt of truth-juice when you can seal yourself off from shared social senses.

"You just know, you know? It's in your gut."

It's maybe how you choose a movie or trim your plants or let the phone just keep ringing.

Maybe it's an efficient and miraculous leap you make between a single grain of rice in your bowl and the totality of the universe culminating in the delivery of that caloric energy from the far reaches of interstellar space into your precise blood stream.

Maybe all of that is contained in a nod of your head or a mumbled word of thanks.

It's maybe something folded into the thump of a pulse.

"We are all star dust."

Other times, a mental desire path is maybe why someone needs to suicide bomb the shopping mall.

26

I left the vanished building site with the stolen package. I walked with it dangling from the tips of my fingers.

My legs lunged me forward beside buildings and under gaps open to the sky. Sunlight warmed my head. Roof-shaped shadows chilled me back into winter.

The package sometimes caught an edge in the air and redirected itself. Aerodynamics. Wind shear. I swung it in rhythm with walking. Moved with it. Adjusted my flow and gate in response to it.

A package in transit. Each of us.

My shoes flashed left right left right into my lower periphery. My right arm swung in counter-balanced sync with my left leg. The envelope's bulk pendulumed at the end of my right hand in echo with my right leg's glide.

Kinetic oppo-positional arcs embodying a front-ward moving quadri-appendaged bi-ped.

A walker with a schizophrenic skip.

And as I moved along, I tried to surmise what was inside the package. I wanted to know what was unknown. What did the bag hold? I made it a little game. I tried to reach behind the envelope's barriers with my mind and imagine its contents. It was a playful test of speculation on the way to getting somewhere I hadn't decided yet.

Determining something indeterminate en route to an unknown destination. An act of knowing while lost. Attempting to see into the hidden by using only what is evident.

A game of deduction. Before time runs out. A popular human pastime. Kind of a variation on Beat the Clock (is that still a game people play?).

The rules of the game became self-evident: could I figure out what was sealed off from direct sensing before reaching a moment when I choose time is up? Before the point at which I open the envelope, could I see into what was obscured and thereby prove knowledge to be knowable?

Could I confirm knowing?

Could I conquer mystery and pack it into the body of understanding?

Could I climb up the delicately balanced sand dune of knowledge and place one more grain of fact on top? Could I secure an answer upon that ever-eroding wreckage? Could I cap that mass with another slain question?

Adventurey metaphors abound.

What a fun way to waste time.

It felt both kind of Romantic and Germanic.

Could I figure what was unknown from what I could know?

These two sides of the world—the hidden and the revealed—are always intimately meeting.

Entwined, they co-create. They mutually define, which basically makes it absurd to call them two sides at all, let alone imagine them as against each other.

The known and unknown are always in collaboration, and they aren't just two. They include me doing my figuring in arrangement with them. "They" are always already "Us."

How could we not all be in this together? Me, the package and the contents of my ignorance. These were the players in my game of knowledge making. Or, rather "human knowledge making," for there is likely no other kind of knowledge.

Human sight, sound, touch, taste, smell and thought. Knowing is a sense as humanly subjective as any of the other senses we've so-far sussed. All are modes of interaction and enactment. Tools making something tooled. Vehicles of transit through time and space.

Trace makers.

Shift shapers.

Risk takers.

Place stakers.

The doors of perception swing between rooms that we assume in order to imagine worlds.

27

Roughly 30cm by 25cm, the light brown envelope was not really smooth to the touch. It had an odd abrasive texture which seemed designed to avoid friction and scratch.

I could see no obvious opening, but yet there was an offered exit: a tiny high-tech pull-tab for unsealing the package. I suspected I could also just cut the thing open. Tearing would take some effort to get through its toughness, but it could be interesting to try.

The contents fit within the package's contours. Of course, they did. That's an obvious but vital fact.

The contents also gave the surface some of its shape. Partly defined it. Whatever was inside gave the outside form its bulk, rise, swells and dips. The limits of one affected the limits of the other. The interior shaped the exterior. And, likely, vice-versa. The two sides made each other.

But, what were the interior structures that created the outside appearance?

What gave the contents their 3D push outward, their density, rigidity and give?

What was inside?

That's what I wanted to know.

And that has long been the quest of humanity.

That was what my game was all about.

I crossed the width of Yotsubashi-suji Street and moved with the north-flowing traffic. The sun touched my right cheek.

Suddenly, inspired by nothing in particular, I decided the destination of my walk.

I decided I'd go until I reached "The Past." I would walk until "The Past" was fulfilled in some form that made the term obviously realized.

I'd go along lost until "The Past" was found.

The rule was made. I liked that.

Up till the "The Past" appeared, I would have my time to try and fathom the invisible.

My random clock was set. Time would be determined by movement towards an unknown point of arrival.

I liked that, too.

I felt the challenge of my private game ignite and excite me. The formality and looseness of it. The trust-wrapped risk towards an outcome.

Each step would launch me out into space and land me in place at the speed of my pace.

A walking game. A game of attentive figuring and inspirational drift. A game each of us who is born into senses and gravity plays. A rickety Rube Goldberg assemblage of assumptions, logics and guesswork.

Making sense, or at least giving it a go.

28

The rectangle of beige paper wasn't just paper. It was obviously some type of special fiber technology. Its texture to my touch and the way it resisted bending felt like it was deeply thought. Some engineer of pulp blends and weaving had surely been running tensile strength tests on hair-thin lengths of spun plant, insect and chemical strands. Elasticity. Rigidity. Frictional slip. Torque resistance.

I envisioned a lab of busy tension-adepts working to develop some tougher variety of the world's most popular actualization of the 2D form: a super paper.

The envelope's sound even reinforced my sense of it having a high-tech pedigree. There was something different to its sound from that of paper paper. When the envelope was squeezed, it made tiny sharp clicks, as though of insistent protest and self-recovery. An audible physical static. Bodily sh-h-h-h. Bit by bit, tick by tick, it was letting me know that it was not giving in. This packaging was not passive. This envelope had evident desires to exceed and do unique things. Fulfill tasks. Store valuables. Transport delicate items. Protect contents entrusted to it.

This was a dutiful container.

I turned left and entered Utsubo Park. I began walking down one of the park's long central paths.

Over the asphalt, a canopy of bare branches from the edging trees cast some spiky shade.

A public toilet stood on my right and I noticed a group of people gathered outside. They were standing around and doing some kind of agility test against the toilet's outside wall. They were fitting their bodies against the building's exterior surface, as though to compare the attributes of one versus the other. The pliable versus the solid. The fleshed skeletal against the tiled concrete. Armatures of response and endurance. The regenerating vs. the erosional.

Not wanting to get too much into their happenings, I just glanced at them before proceeding on, letting the envelope motivate my progress.

I felt the package with my hands as I moved along. I squeezed and tilted and warped it. While lightweight, the contents of the package seemed complex. A soft assemblage of many pieces, or several of several. Too solid to be liquid. Too flexible to be brittle. Too flat to be folded. Too soft to be sharp.

The assertions of absences.

The mass inside exerted its existence on the outside through such negative signs, through a language of logical exclusions.

The contents created a few obvious bulges without much density.

A pliant resistance. Fluffy, boingy, smushy.

As well, I could feel that whatever was inside would shift slightly as I leaned the buff-colored rectangle one way or another.

Obviously, gravity could reach beyond the exterior surface of the envelope and play on the mass inside. What was inside didn't escape from those absolute forces. The earth played its inclusive role everywhere, even inside this envelope.

As well, the contents moved within the internal space that maintained them. They shifted inside those dimensions of up/down and back/forth. They were mostly limited to those 2 dimensions by the lack of depth. Another deceptively important obviousness.

The contents were free, but not fully. Space kept them assembled. They fit within the pressures that sustained them as they were. Even if the contents were removed from this outside atmosphere, they had their own atmospheric pressures to deal with. So, while secluded from the outer world, the contents were not fully beyond. Gravity had its influence. As did mass and two of space's typical dimensions. Lacking much 3D thrust, the contents pushed outward while they were held in.

Maybe 2.5D.

Space. Atmosphere. Gravity. Dimension.

Not much different from us wrapped-up animated packages walking around out here.

Skin keeps us contained and shaped. Without the atmosphere and gravity, we'd explode out and disperse into space's vacuum.

However, sound did not exceed the package's wall. I couldn't hear anything from inside. No scrape or squeak or gurgle.

The contents were mute. Or, muted. Either because of the surface or some silencing secret also hidden inside that space, I couldn't hear any sound from within the envelope. The only sound was the sibilant scrape and textured clicks the package's paper whispered against my pressing and rub.

As well, I couldn't tell if smell was able to make it outside. Maybe the contents didn't have any.

As I sniffed the outside surface of the package, there was a hint of fragrance—some note of sweetness. But, it seemed to be possibly from the stain that covered the corner near the post mark's stamp. Could that stain be from some spill of perfume or juice? Could the scent be from the stamp's red ink? Could the super-paper release a scent when touched by water, some other liquid or excessive probing? Was the scent a security measure? A scratch-n-sniff signal of potential tampering?

The paper was obviously undamaged by the stain, except for showing the curved jagged edge of whatever liquid had touched it. A trace of a moment in time when some unknown agent made contact. Probably not recently.

The ink of the nearly ten-month-old postmark was slightly blurred in the area of the stain. Perhaps that happened in the postman's rainy day delivery, but it could equally be from some other time during the package's long wait in the stuffed mailbox.

It's hard to determine an answer because the imagination can go on forever in such hypotheses.

But I can say with certainty that the super-paper obviously did its protective duty well.

29

As I moved through Utsubo Park, I noticed a long white line of chalk on the ground. It was about as wide as the envelope was long, but made up of rows of parallel stripes. A white line made up of white lines.

I paused and followed it with my eyes. I saw there was another white line on the parallel path that also ran the length of the park. Two straight paths with a 30cm chalk line running down each.

Lines made of lines made of lines. Intriguing.

The chalk was thick and clumped in places, but in other spots thin and barely there.

As I followed the lines, I saw two groups of people. One was at the end of each white line.

Each group was clustered together in focused operation around a large rolling object. Each group was moving slowly as it operated its object, so I followed and quickly caught up with them without walking too much faster.

I approached and saw that each object was a large rubber tire about a meter in diameter. Two black rubber airplane wheels, each being rolled by a team. They were printing chalk traces in their passage.

Each team was made of five operators. Two members balanced and rolled the wheel using a horizontal axel. One member walked backwards in front of the wheel and coated it with chalk while the last two carried buckets of dry white powder and recharged the brushes that were then handed back to the backward-pacing painter. All of this effort kept the line extending.

Each of the members was dressed in what looked like a flight suit of vague national association from the WWII era, but the uniforms' vibrancies were artfully drained of almost all color, as though the life in the insignias, ranks and fabrics had been sucked out by ghosts of aphasia.

Each operator also had a passport-sized card hanging from their neck with a few words explaining what they were doing.

The card said they had each made a "promise of silence." In addition, the card stated that Utsubo Park had been a US military air strip built after much of Osaka was destroyed in bombings in 1945. The runway was the reason for the park's unique long shape.

When close enough to read the cards, I was also able to notice that their flight suits were not merely—or even actually—faded cloth. They were in fact made of printed images of cities bombed in wars. Arial POVs. Street-level shots. Interiors of twisted girders and rubble. Rivers shining through leveled quadrangles of ruined streets. Dust drifts obscuring precariously leaning apartment buildings. Crossroad intersections orbited by the vacant black satellites of bomb-pocks.

Whether on ink-jetted paper, antique postcard prints, or photocopies of old Life Magazine issues, the image-scraps were sewn together to make well-wrought uniforms that only gave away their secrets up-close. Images of cities driven back to bare ground. Surfaces shattered until they exposed their usually encased soils to the sunlight, rain and wind.

The images captured moments when places became spaces and were thus open to the brutal logics of when powers-that-be grab and give and beat back the dying with shrugs. In such nowheres, survivors learn the efficacy of amnesia.

The plane wheels kept rolling through the park.

I didn't ask if this was a commemoration, a regular gesture or a one-time spasm of resurrecting memory. I just popped a pair of flu-capsules into my throat and paced slowly along while watching the turning wheels.

I watched the white powder move from the buckets to the treads and then to the ground. Again and again. When a wind would occasionally flirt through the park, puffs of white line would rise up in spots and swirl into the bare winter trees.

Localized clouds of past purposes, as though memories held by the park were being triggered to arise like smoke off a gasping ember.

I took one such cloud as a direction-giver and followed its drift to the northwest.

The cloud pointed out a line through a narrow forest in the park. I followed it and came to a span of greenish grass. I stopped and considered my options to get to the other side.

To my right, there was a curving paved footpath that was designed to let me stroll amidst various displays of rose bushes before getting to the far side of the lawn. To my left was a straight and narrow dirt track worn through the grass by regular foot traffic. The dirt track led directly over a low hill and towards an exit from the park.

Envelope and stick in hand, I took the desire path.

30

Exiting the north side of Utsubo Park, I moved amidst the rhythms of corporate lunch times. Groups of business-suited men and women flowed in directions driven by desires of the tongue. To eat and talk. To refuel bodies and exorcise morning office gripes.

I tapped my stick to try and attract some confused looks, but they were not even interested in looking for traffic much less at a foreign form feigning blindness.

I tucked the package beneath my arm and proceeded past a small sun-filled parking lot. An elderly man was leaning his oddly angulated body against the side wall of a corporate distributer of colorful fruit juices.

Why he was doing that to the wall, I didn't know. I pondered for a moment. Was he measuring his body against the architecture or trying to heal some rebellion of back muscles? Was he checking himself for abilities or charting a litany of declines?

The wind blew and I noticed another wisp of white chalk dust in the air. I followed it away from the old guy.

Moving by signs, scents and surmising pointers, I might as well have been just going lost or grasping after wayward angels.

But then, not long after, I knew I had arrived.

On a bending backstreet in an area I could never find again, "The Past" became embodied.

I'd gotten to where I was going.

Nostalgia was cast in proudly patinaed bronze. A past day in a past sun when a past moment forever marked the hearts of some—or at least the heart of someone with enough money to build this.

Over the fence of a wedged-in parking lot was a small private sanctuary of statues. Without any noticeable public entrance, the little backyard park enshrined a moment of baseball. Was it a specific historic event? Was it a general scene symbolizing qualities embodied by the sport? Was it an individual's private memory that refused forgetting?

I still don't know for sure.

But, it was "The Past" I'd been looking for.

31

The baseball shrine was an empty space of well-kept grass and three pieces of sculpture. Other than that, no answers. Just a bunch of interpretive hints.

On the left was a sculpture of four fold-down stadium seats that were positioned looking out over the grass field. Not far from them to the right, a larger-than-life-sized bronze catcher stood. He is caught forever removing his mask as though to watch a home run ball fly over the fence and beyond the limits of play. His gloved hand blocks the sun from his eyes. The catcher dutifully lets the moment etch defeat into his heart. He lets his heart exceed his hopes for victory and stretch out into the elastic dimensions of despair.

This was not the portrayal of a happy time, but it was obviously a moment filled with potentials, meanings and values. The moment's importance was made evident through the amount of effort someone made to solidify it into sculptured metal.

The catcher holds onto that moment as an important one. The player who symbolically receives all that is thrown at him, catches a moment when a time before became a time after. The catcher embodies the moment when a hope became a defeat.

And the final piece of sculpture in the triptych stands to the right of the catcher.

It is of a home base umpire. Placed near the catcher, the umpire appears to be like a priest whose presence validates the pseudo-random rules of the game—the three strikes, four balls, four bases, three outs, etc. The umpire activates vague psychic powers that are generated by the game's structures of play. The game becomes a medium of reality under the sincere enforcement of its rules, and thus a judge is needed. A reality requires the enforcement and respect of limitations. With judgement, play becomes ritual action, capable of shaping emotional impacts. A game becomes serious. Time takes direction. A fair-flying ball that goes beyond the limits of the field of play triggers the end of a ritual effort and identifies who are winners and who are losers. Determinators.

The umpire's judgement marks a momentous event, fixes time and fragments of selves into places. The umpire's ruling affects value.

Life changing stuff.

I stood there feeling transfixed by the scene.

I peered through the metal bars of the fence at the rather weird baseball shrine. I blankly looked at the sculptures and let the objects weave together their strands of meaning into a rather open narrative.

I absorbed their assertions, allusions and pleas.

Then, I remembered that I was standing in a small parking lot.

I scurried out of the way as a tiny white car came backing in and its driver hopped out. This brought me back to the there and then.

The driver slammed the car door and dashed across the street towards a company's warehouse. A number of employees were milling around in their uniforms, chatting and smoking. As well, a woman who seemed to be looking for directions on her phone drifted near the building's corner. Beyond there, other people strolled the area's streets in post-lunch stupors.

I was all alone in my world while parallel worlds hummed along on their own.

As though time had been briefly suspended, the envelope that unconsciously dangled from my hand reconnected me to what I was doing.

I had a purpose. My game with the envelope was now over.

I had arrived at the time I was looking for. "The Past" had appeared. Now, it was time to check my answer to the question of what was inside the bag.

32

Looking at the envelope, I had developed a degree of respect for it and now I had mixed feelings about opening it. It had been doing its job of securing its contents for almost a year. The envelope showed its commitment to duty, so I felt kind of guilty about ending its efforts.

Of course, this wasn't really my package to open anyway. It wasn't addressed to me. I'd removed it from the mailbox on a whim, or perhaps my kleptomaniac desires had randomly flared up. I hadn't really had any interest in having what was inside. I'd merely been oddly attracted to the package. It was a spur thing. A reactive act of theft.

Only later on, during my walk, did I playfully wonder if I could determine what was inside the envelope. This whole game was just an afterthought of my *petit* crime.

And I partly knew that to actually know the contents would spoil something, spoil the beautiful openness of the wondering. Knowing the answer would kill the vibrancy of the question.

When the envelope is opened, I would be clearly and definitely determined and affirmed as right or wrong. No vague hope for the virtual's lurking potential. There'd be an answer, an empirical truth. An actualized proof. And the openness of the playtime would be finished.

An end would happen. The game would be dead and the answer would be its corpse: its pulseless, rotting and odorous corpse. The question's ghost might mutter some circular wish of what could have occurred in various imaginary trajectories, but all those "maybes" would lack the life of the genuine unknown. They would pale in comparison. The ghost's drone would just be the sad litany of "What if."

But, the eventual need for action always arrives.

Delay comes to an end.

The cut has to be made.

If I did nothing, what was I supposed to not do next?

As my father used to sometimes say, like a magic spell to break us kids out of paralysis: "Do something, even if it's wrong."

So, I decided to just play out the game.

I had reached what I knew was "The Past." And so, I looked for a memorable way to open the envelope.

33

I've learned that when something has to change, it's best to make an event of it. Let it find its own unique way to breathe its last gasp. I've learned to let outside players join in on a condition's demise. There are always collaborators on hand to augment the context and let a memory shiver rather than just pose quietly.

Such rites give the ghost of what's lost more of a voice to sing with, rather than just emit a whimper that will scratch inside the future. Such rites direct how elements of futures collect, connect and correct what comes after. The past becomes a semi-autonomous agent. A change becomes able to entangle future conditions if it sticks out a bit at excited or activated angles. Making something an event gives the past more tentacles and suction cups with which it can wriggle amidst and cling to what is not yet.

The past is never really stored safely in a box on some shelf in some mental self-storage unit. The past is always lurking between present moments. It isn't over. It frames the new. It inflects and infects and unfolds.

The past rushes up with a needle to prick or sew.

The past shuttles between intensities of the now and then.

The past exerts its own desires.

So, standing in that little car park, I looked at the envelope in my hand. I leaned my multi-colored stick against the fence and then I looked for something sharp to help me make opening the envelope an evocation.

I wanted to find some spike or hook or jagged edge with which I could impale or saw the super-paper open. I didn't want to just pull the envelope's open tab. I walked around the parking lot, looking at car bumpers and protruding tree roots.

And then, there on the bottom corner of the statue park's fence, I found a blade-in-waiting. A corner weld had rusted undone but the steel's angle was still smooth and sharp enough for my need.

I touched my finger to it and could feel its brilliant capacity to slice.

I put the long edge of the envelope up to the "blade," a couple centimeters from its top corner. I gripped the envelope's long edge with my right hand and the top corner with my left. I abruptly jerked it crosswise once to start a slit, and then quickly glided the envelope's width over the clean shearing steel. A smooth singular sound.

Not a tear and not a cut. A slash.

I could never do that again. It was the agile perfection of first-timing-it. An opening of unique consequences.

34

After being slashed open, the envelope seemed to almost pause to think, as though it was resisting change or preparing to make a public statement. Surely this effect was caused by some vacuumed interior environment that was processing its abrupt interaction with the outside world.

The closed was confronting the open.

After the initial moments, I could hear some kind of process taking place at the site of the cut. It was preparing its voice of protest. Energies were interacting and negotiating new conditions. New balances were being sussed and struck. The sound was of intensities becoming other, and this process required much more energy to be expended than I had thought possible from a high-tech sack.

I can best describe it as a crackle of muttering differences, some kind of highly expressive drone of complaint. And the sound was loud enough that it attracted the attention of people across the road who were on the final cusp of their lunch break. Men in front of the building let cigarette butts drop and started to drift my way across the small backstreet.

The woman at the corner stayed there, but her gaze was secretly all in.

I watched the cut.

Whatever was inside was very hostile to the outside world bridging the slit. The lips of the envelope vibrated like a double-reeded flute, producing a whine of crackling vibrations. The tone slipped and jerked, shifting from a low growl to a piercing screech depending on the amount of edge beating against itself.

And gradually a cloud developed, localized to the site of this siren turbulence.

At first the cloud seemed just like a heat vapor, producing a rippling but transparent blur. But as the drone built its range of layered expression, the cloud took on a faint pink.

The men approaching saw this cloud clearly and stopped in a sudden caution, putting their hands out in protection and turning their bodies slightly to instinctively keep vital organs safe.

They inched closer, repeatedly voicing the sounds of mystery. The gasps and awes and huhs that homo sapiens have always grunted when facing the What The Fuck.

The company workers approached, muttering the tones of questioning reality.

The envelope was shaking in my hands as though whatever was inside had woken up and was stirring to reactions.

The weight inside the bag shifted back and forth, becoming almost hard to handle. Pushed from one limit to another limit, the contents seemed to flee into a protective corner and then search out another. Finding no escape, they then rushed towards the slit as though to confront the invading difference head-on. But, the contents never made it out during this whole period of volatile rebalancing. Something blocked their emergence.

And through it all, the pink cloud gathered into a more intensely pink pink.

However, ultimately and eventually, any inside is only a fragment of an outer expanse, and all rebellions are finally absorbed by the broader ambivalent calm. So, over time, the bag became quiet.

The envelope had inhaled a considerable amount of the outside and become almost buoyant. The contents were still contained inside but were now docile or dead. A taming or acquiescence had taken place. The broader world had instilled its logic.

But the cloud remained, as though magnetically attracted to the cut. The trace of what had passed continued to glow.

35

The mouth of the bag was now quiet and relaxed. It yawned open.

I tried to look inside the bag, but the cloud more than blurred. It obscured. The only options I had were to either reach in or pour out.

[My choice will tell you what kind of heart I have.]

I tilted the bag slightly and tapped its edge, urging the insides to take gravity at its offer.

I could tell the onlookers were in a state of conflict. Their lunch break was surely over by now, but this was not an everyday event. Most of them heeded the clock, but two of them stayed. Their eyes remained fixed on the unpredictable details taking place.

I tilted and tapped. I tilted more and tapped a bit more intensely. I could feel the insides began to shift, but the cloud continued to cling to the bag's opening, as though the cloud's presence was a final buffer keeping the past in place.

But when I tilted the envelope beyond all obvious resistance, the cloud floated down, as though pushed away by the weight of the exiting contents.

Out of the bag fell pink flower after pink flower after pink flower.

At times they fell by ones. At times, a grouped few. Each flower was about a hand's palm across and made of five vivid pink petals assembled around a central crown of golden tuft. I lost count, but maybe there were 10 to 15.

And, as they fell from the mouth of the bag towards the cloud hovering below, each was perfect and fragrant. But as they approached the edge of the cloud, they began to immediately decay and dissolve. As though their year in the bag was catching up to them in a moment, the petals passed through the cloud and reemerged as a cascade of brown dust which fell to the ground in a pile of powdered detritus.

The slacker-workers, woman at the corner and I were all spell-bound.

No one spoke, except for one worker who once said, "Memory dust," midway through the process.

I continued to hold the bag, not knowing if all the flowers had fallen out yet.

After waiting for nothing, I tried to look inside the envelope again and this caused the cloud to release and drift.

It floated up to my face and caught me in the middle of an inhalation, filling my head with a scent that immediately buckled my knees.

I fell to the blacktop and could barely keep from tipping over onto my face. My hands went out and I heard the sound of the bag scratching the asphalt under them. My eyes glazed and the sky went liquid.

Then the spinning spun for who knows how many panting breaths.

While I was lost in that swirl of time, I experienced a tumbling replay of my last year's forgettings.

I have no way to organize the memories I saw except to say that they were all-at-once. The experience could have unfolded in the time it took me to fall over and then look up, or I could have been down there for a year systematically reliving all the deleted minutia that had passed into my short-term memory and been immediately discarded as noise.

Coins clinking into return trays.

Tangles of electric wires running from outlets to devices.

Trash can mouths and their sculptural assemblages of garbage.

Wrinkles on necks.

Strangers talking and others responding.

Tape on the cardboard box containing Cadere's skin.

Leaves en masse slightly shifting in breezes.

Doors and knobs.

My foot steps.

Street sounds.

Coffee in cups.

Ankles flexing and propelling women up stairs.

A film about endangered animals.

Things in front of things in front of things, all providing contextual foregrounds and backgrounds for my focal eye.

A dog's dash across a street.

A man's fingers pushing his face in rest.

Rain running down a drain.

36

In cities there are things called ghost streets.

Perhaps best visible on maps, they are where an edge of a previous layout of buildings or an extinct road continues to exert its trajectory amidst the current topography. A fold showing through from an old form which a new pattern has subsumed—but only almost.

A ghost street is a trace from the past that preserves itself within the assertions of the present, at least for now.

A ghost street can be an element that's not gone yet, but is fading like a healing wound or decaying scar. It might be a diagonal alley from an earlier time's urban planning that cuts through a neighborhood of rigidly straight and perpendiculated streets. It might be an off-kilter alignment of building walls and property fencing from some old arrangement of lots that reveals itself in contrast as it slices odd-cocked and crooked across a new area of copied-n-pasted squared-up city blocks.

Ghost streets are a past logic contending with a now.

A ghost street might be an irregularly wiggling gap meandering between property lines, evidence of what once was maybe a small waterway but is now only kept in existence by illogically zigzagging yard boarders or an extended length of unowned and untended hedge-growth dividing landlorded plots from other landlorded plots.

A cat track.

A trash-gathering pathway.

A no man's land.

Depending on its size, a former creek—likely long since dry or filled in—might become a narrow stroll-way that nobody claims. A wild tract. A habitat for possums and rats. A dog shit stretch. A garbage-laden passage where various forms of lesser pedestrians slink between land-ends and proper properties.

A ghost street is a place between places, semi-invisible and uninviting.

An escape route through overgrowth too narrow or tangled for pursuers to chase.

A space too worthless to eradicate or battle for in court.

A useless run of ugliness.

An abandoned gap between purposeful dreams.

An afterthought, or a prethought gone to rot.

A blank page left in history.

Unexposed frames in a film which flash past unnoticed but offer spaces for imagining all sorts of impossible lives.

A vacuum for specters and speculative logics.

A crawl space.

A worm hole.

A DMZ: A DeMeaninged Zone.

37

Lying on the parking lot pavement, I don't really know how long I was lost amidst my annual amnesic litany. But, it must not have been too long. When I became aware of the present moment again, the pink cloud was still maintaining its shape. I saw it floating above me like a threat, so I kept close to the ground.

Sunlight played in brief eclipse behind its edge.

Gradually the wind found ways to shift the cloud's form and dispersed the concentrated scent of the flowers' past. The odor spread into the city's ever-open willingness to accept all such strange and toxic compilations.

The cloud's smell was like a pungent burst of the concentrated life that it had absorbed off the pink flowers.

I guess.

Or, perhaps it was their death.

I can't say I know for sure either way.

After having the cloud saturate my sinuses, I can only honestly say that I smell hints of it in everything ever since. Either because the smell is always with me now, or because everything contains some of that distinct fragrance and now I have a reference for recognizing something that has always been.

I shifted to all-fours and looked around. Everybody was gone. What happened to them? Had they ever even been there? Wouldn't they try to see if I was okay? Were rescue personnel on their way?

If so—and regardless—I decided I should get up and get out of there.

I picked up my stick and tried to jog the scent off. I quickly got tired and just walked.

I carried the envelope for a short while but thought I should get rid of it somehow.

Discard any evidence.

As I walked beside the west wall of a YMCA, I scraped the envelope's surface against the rough stucco. The label with the envelope's addressee quickly ground into white specks. They fell like dandruff and vanished on micro-breezes.

I detoured into a small parking lot that was fit into a blank space between buildings. The far end of the parking lot was made by the wall shoring up the southern bank of Osaka's Tosabori River, the south river forming Nakanoshima Island.

I approached the parking lot's stained and scarred wall. It was decorated with traces of glue and messages of varying degrees of life and validity. A piece of crap graffiti. A faded political poster for an election from five years before. The poster's saggy-faced, square-headed would-be district representative forced a smile into place and held up a weak fist.

Did he ever win? What was he ready to weakly fight for? Was he even still alive?

A torn flyer for a circus fluttered, its date and contact information missing. A small lone poster for something called Zujaka that was to occur at 8pm. But, no information was given about the location, date, type of event and even what Zujaka was.

Just a statement of existence. An announced being. Vague, formless and luring.

In addition, there was a rusty, painted sign warning children about the dangers of under-age smoking. The hand-painted image featured a crying child being lorded over by a *yakuza* henchman in dark sunglasses gesturing the energies of intimidation. He had a mashed-dead cigarette in his hand. The child's face was full of regret, panic and despair. A group of disappointed teachers watched from the background. The *Yak*'s dynamic body language threatened violence if cash wasn't offered up immediately.

That drama would last forever, as universal as rust.

I wedged the rectangle of super-paper envelope behind the metal sign of melodrama, letting it protect a different kind of minor crime.

I popped a small green gel-cap for nasal drip and departed.

38

After leaving the little parking lot, I continued walking through streets. I moved from one square island of shadow to another with brief flights through whatever sunlight could find the asphalt.

Edging the river's line, the side streets became smaller and the buildings got taller. I strolled along an alley that echoed the Tosabori's curve and came to a cross street heading up and over the river.

I turned left and climbed a slight incline leading up onto Chikuzen Bridge. I glimpsed the water rippling in its flow. Then, at one point in the rise to the sidewalk, I could see through a narrow break in the clutter of concrete infrastructure and got a brief view of the bridge's steel understructure. A little peek-gap.

I stopped and stared.

There, under the bridge, I looked at what seemed to be a red shape painted onto one of the bridge's supporting grey I-beams. I couldn't make sense of the red image at first. Was it a *kanji* character or part of a graffitied word? Was it just an abstract red blob? It was hard to tell.

But, then I realized that the flatness of the image was an illusion.

Because my view was so obscured, I was not able to see the red shape with both eyes. I had no depth perception. My stereo-optic vision had been flattened down into only 2D. But, as I looked, the painting moved. What I had first seen to be a piece of graffiti sprayed under the bridge was actually a small person. The red shape moved and that gave it away. There was someone doing something under the bridge.

Graffiti doesn't climb around or make its bed.

I stopped fully and kept myself hidden behind the bridge's large concrete anchor. This suddenly felt less like looking and more like spying. The object became a subject.

I watched as a person who was dressed all in red moved around on the ironwork under the bridge. The person wore a hooded sweatshirt which obscured his or her head.

The color was a red I can only describe as red/orange, some elemental hue of fire. And with pants to match. But unless my ability to determine size was as tweaked as my ability to read 3D had been, this person was only about a meter tall. Could it be a child under there? Was it a man? A woman? A midget? A dressed-up monkey? A ghost?

All these questions went through my mind.

The person moved smoothly and easily within the bridge's support beams, seemingly organizing something that was kept up there. The movements felt like the gestures of making a bed, with obvious skill and attention to detail.

Does he live in there? Is that her sleeping spot?

As I watched, I could feel he was preparing to leave. She was looking around the steel beams and checking that things were in place. Then, he lowered herself down to a horizontal girder beneath his "bed" and moved towards the outer edge of the bridge.

She looked out quickly and immediately made eye-contact with me, but showed no sign of surprise or concern. He looked up toward the area of the bridge's road surface and then swung her body out and smoothly climbed up to the railing above.

I was right. The person was tiny. As he came to the street level and slipped over the railing, I could see her scale relative to the street furniture.

He was shorter than the railing's height. But the person did not move like a child, nor have the face of a child. The person was not young, but I could not determine a gender from her face or his movements. A midget?

The only thing I could be sure of was her incredible agility to move through those spaces. This was his environment, one she'd obviously lived within for a long time.

As soon as he got over the railing, the person transformed into a decrepit cripple, bent over severely, with extreme trouble moving. Limping and shuffling between one spot and the next.

Was this an act? Why? The fluidity and sinewy ease within the bridge's understructure vanished and was replaced by a wobbling disability. She doddered tentatively towards the far side of the bridge, planting a battered cane for support each pace of the way.

Where'd the cane suddenly come from?

The arch of the bridge obscured my view at one point, so I moved up to see more.

But now he was gone. I followed up onto the middle of the bridge but couldn't find any trace. I continued across the bridge and checked the gutter grates and under parked cars, but saw no sign of her.

I chose a direction from there and continued looking as I went east on the north side of the south river, but still found no indication of him having been that way.

I suspected that there was a secret escape route that would be visible and obvious if I knew how to look. But I didn't know how to see exits from that area edging the Tosabori river's northern embankment wall. I could only see rusty chainlink fencing, cropped grass and strewn trash.

I was just a typical pedestrian. I had no special ability to find the doors that were likely present. I could not read the secrets that were surely obvious for her to escape through. I couldn't tell what scratched mark or stack of broken wooden pallets indicated a hiding spot or the entrance into a private vein through the city.

I had the sense there was something there that the red hooded person was adept at using. But I didn't know how to sense that sense, let alone translate it into knowing.

39

Walking on, I stopped searching for his/her portals into some hidden city of the city.

The worst way to find something, for me, is to look for it too intently.

Instead, I just wandered and tapped tapped tapped.

I used my stick and scratched my way along, giving a little rap to things I came across. I didn't close my eyes, but rather just tapped the tip of the stick against anything that looked resonant.

Like a doctor thumping on a bared body to listen for secrets beneath the skin, I tested the street's surfaces. Beyond its outer layers, I found echoes, sounds, noises and musics.

It didn't take long for me to start imagining what was inside and beneath the city's skin and its bolted-down street gear. Its voids, volumes and cavities. Its recessed meter box lids and bridge struts. Its drain covers and locked traffic control cabinets. All of them responded to percussive touches. Some dull and some brilliant and some almost sing-songy.

And from below the streets, the town's sounds answered. My taps echoed back from hidden hollows and stirred degrees of the city's surfaces' densities.

The city's skin vibrated and hummed. Each surface spoke with its own voice.

Iron gutter-grates ping or pong.

Vinyl meter hatches bunt or boom.

Metal manhole covers ring, ting, gong or thud.

And the unseen dimensions they each prevent access to play a part in making their sounds.

I could guess at the size and shapes of the spaces beyond. I could read those hidden spaces from how they responded to my taps.

Each secreted space had its own tells to my taps.

I went down into the subway and checked the floors of an underground hallway and a pedestrian passage. They resonated with different thicknesses. The firmnesses of any floor are various and locational. They are supported from beneath and no place is the same everywhere. Floors might look uniform, but their voices tell of reinforcements, sub-structures and hidden holes.

As well, floor tiles click, clonk and at times even clong. Their materials have accent and nuance.

Things express.

The smooth concretes and the rough concretes and the spray-sealed concretes.

The echoey gorgeousness of bridges and their railings.

I tapped all I came across.

Alleys ring and ricochet from pedestrian heels.

A tunnel is a world of surround-sound immersion.

The city is richly layered of such percussive songs.

So, I started thinking of my stick as a tool, a tapping spear. Like a phonographic stylus reveals the sounds grooved into a vinyl record, I nicknamed my stick "The Needle."

With it I transphoned the city's surfaces into audible tones.

As I continued walking, I thought about installing a contact microphone and a cable-jack onto The Needle so I could record or amplify what the stick sensed. Lost in wandering thought, I envisioned someday giving performances of different acoustic walks, dragging The Needle across streets and along grooves divined amidst pavement stones. I imagined tapping metal covers and other echoing emitters of clang as an audience of wonderment-lost followers listened.

I could "play" the textures of the city.

I could tap a famous road or a certain fascinating neighborhood.

Then I realized I was being followed.

Hear this Book: Be a Needle

* Close this book.
* Place the front cover against your ear.
* Run your finger tip around inside the black rectangle printed on the back cover.
* Translate the book's audio statement into something you understand.

40

Do you remember the parking lot where I had inhaled the flowers' hallucination? Do you remember that I noticed a woman who seemed to be openly hiding? Or, I could say she was hiding by being too obviously there. Remember her? She was standing next to the building's corner and her body was turned at a suitable angle to both observe and obscure. I can say she had a consciousness of watching her own consciousness. She had an intensity of diverted attention.

Well, she was back and I realized she was following me.

I first renoticed her down a backstreet south of the river. Then again in the subway hallway. Then another time leaning against a lamp post.

Maybe in her 40s. Thin. A bit shorter than me, she wore a blue-striped white shirt under a green khaki coat that came down to below mid-thigh. A little rumpled and slouchy, it was a jacket a TV detective would wear. A jacket that seemed a bit too big for her, as though she'd borrowed or inherited it from a male friend. Not a fashionable coat, but obviously familiar and trusted. Pocket space for hands and notes.

When I became sure she was following me, she was one street over from my street. She was walking in the same direction as me but without her own direction. Short steps, but at a pace that kept pace with my pace. She was attuning to my movements. Watching me without watching.

I'd see her at times and then not see her.

She was obviously on my tail, but I didn't mind.

I didn't care. I just kept tapping tapping tapping.

It was hard to know if she was wearing a long narrow skirt or rather short loose trousers. Her short steps made it hard to tell. Without seeing any divided legs, I couldn't tell what in her clothes was flow or what was separation.

She wore a knit cap, and glasses that seemed to change their tint in different lights.

A total spy look, if you ask me. Like someone spying on herself, even if on no one else. A hobby stalker. A sorter of details. A list maker and fan of Venn diagrams. She looked like someone looking to cull overlaps of vital data.

She was a woman moving within secrets, but not so good at hiding that fact.

Then, I lost sight of her.

Or, she caught on and tried to throw me off her trailing.

So, when I saw her again outside the Toray building, I knew for sure that she was there in wait. There was no doubt anymore.

I knew there was going to be contact made. A "hit" or a photo snapped or an "Excuse me," before she probably broke into a list of questions.

I wouldn't initiate it, but it would happen. To the security cameras, it would look awkward but like chance.

She looked awkward but like chance.

Knowing something was coming, I tried to enjoy being hunted.

41

There was a Starbucks in the Toray building's lobby. The Starbucks was what consumed most people's attention there.

That is the reason for a Starbucks' existence most anywhere, right?

The drink posters and enthusiastic cashiers provide a reassuring comfort of admittance. The acknowledged cost of feeling welcomed by strangers. The confident products promise creative insights and corporate promotion.

White-collar sparkle.

The Starbucks in the Toray lobby was a stand-alone glass box of coffee and sugary scents set within the vacuous rising sky of the office building's foyer. This Starbucks never had to suffer from rain, wind or any other turmoil of unpredictability. It was ever-drenched by the pulsing shimmer of fluorescent lights which saturated the space and bounced their particulates/waves into every hiding spot where a shadow might try to abide.

The wider lobby of the Toray building was textured grey granite. Polished grey granite. Rounded grey granite pillars. Squared-off, brushed stainless-steel handles, railings and fixtures. Everything else was architectural glass arranged to wall-in the space.

But, there was also an open secret in the Toray building's lobby space, which was why I still return there.

At the top of a glass escalator that rises up to a wall-less floor right above the Starbucks, there is a nice open sitting space furnished with not uncomfortable black chairs.

Probably intended as a place where businessmen in the building can meet clients, the lounge is a rare free public comfort. Actually, semi-public, because it is surely controlled by the building.

Corporate public.

The lobby is open to foot traffic, so the lounge feels accessible and available, like a gift for urban nomads. And, because the lounge's sparse existence is obscured by the hyper-magnetic power of the Starbucks, the lounge is often empty.

It's a nice place to think, read or lurk.

It has a vibe of privacy, of being a secret space. But it is open, letting anyone access its cushioned chairs to sit, covertly sip and consider.

It is a suspiciously nice space.

And, while I am always ready for a building security guard to possibly appear and gesture at me to get out, that has not yet occurred. The lounge is a pleasantly perpetual perk for my city wandering, and I always wonder if it will still exist the next time I go.

Like life, while it lasts I enjoy the comforts it offers. Reading and just watching the world from a soft black semi-sofa is better than a wooden bench or the usual floor-and-only-the-floor.

42

On the day of my walking/stalking, the lobby of the Toray building provided chances for some very interesting contemplations. I went up, found a chair and watched life play out. But, not just my life.

The lobby was busy with foot traffic on that day, which made the lounge a very good place for watching people, not limited to observing my stalker.

Men and women of the business variety pranced or trudged through the foyer. Each transmitting an evident little drama that bubbled beneath their work face. Briefcases swinging. Bundles of business papers swaddled like a newborn. Each person was moving between froms and tos.

But the lobby also had its own unique blue river of literature.

This was another thing that made the Toray lobby particularly nice.

On the opposite side from the lounge-above-the-Starbucks, the lobby had a contemporary art piece featuring an endless flow of semi-proverbial sayings. Resonating clusters of text would emerge as a constantly crawling line of digital blue words moving along a long, curved message board.

It was a text-based artwork called *Truisms* by Jenny Holzer.

Along a long narrow crawl-screen, short sentences born of blue LED lights wove in and out of sight behind the granite pillars. The English sentences flowed like shining snakes winding through the lobby's space. Every letter was capitalized.

The speed of the flow was both slow enough and too fast to really read. It created some kind of line of urgency that tangled the layers of literal, critical, ironic and cynical meanings into each other and made it feel like some extra element was being smuggled into my logical brain through the process.

The piece had a $1 + 2 + 1 = 5$ feeling.

Some emergent germ that eroded something in the sum.

Some addition that subtracted.

Assassin facts.

The texts stirred some enzyme in my brain that lets confidence blossom at the same time as it freezes it into fakery.

Believable doubts.

Trusted lies.

Parasite proverbs.

Thought bombs with short fuses.

Catch copy for social implosion.

Sitting back in my black chair, I leaned my colorfully striped stick against the glassed edge of the lounge. I sat and watched as the flowing blue texts appeared and disappeared behind the stick.

[MUCH WAS DECIDED BEFORE YOU WERE BORN.]

I typed a note into my phone.

Soon enough, the stalker-woman came into view on the lobby floor.

Her body's speed signaled she'd spotted me too.

She didn't look my way, which made it obvious she was noting my location and determining her modes of access, approach and escape.

The hunt was on.

[MURDER HAS ITS SEXUAL SIDE.]

She feigned reading the blue flow of Holzer phrases. She paused and her head panned as the sayings moved. Shuffling and tilting her head, she repositioned herself. She started walking and I could tell she was planning to arc wide around to her right in order to ride the escalator up to the roof lounge.

Her speed decreased and she avoided looking up, so I knew she was watching. Her trajectory angled into her arc.

From my seat, I stood up and collected my stick off the glass. That was a dramatic move on my part.

She didn't stop, but her angle went straight, as though the source of her orbit had suddenly vanished.

[NOTHING UPSETS THE BALANCE OF GOOD AND EVIL.]

She proceeded slowly, going straight.

Then, I moved to an empty chair two chairs closer to the more secluded corner end of the lounge. That would be better for her.

I could sense her tabulate this. It would be easier for her to cut off my escape, if that's what she hoped. Fish in a bucket logic.

My new gravity engaged her right-revolving orbit again and she took out a thermos to signal a narrative of thirst or a well deserved break time: Oh, look, an elevator to a lounge. What a nice surprise. How convenient.

[PEOPLE ARE BORING UNLESS THEY'RE EXTREMISTS.]

I read the flow of words on the screen, but none of the meanings registered. My mind was flooded with what this woman could be up to. Speculative data crunching. What was going to happen? Was the end approaching? Or was this just leading to an awkward conversation?

[PLANNING FOR THE FUTURE IS ESCAPISM.]

She topped the escalator and began moving with clear intention.

The ruse was over and her focused approach towards me was something the surveillance cameras could clearly document. I didn't turn toward her or look, but I could tell as she approached that she was watching a screen on her phone.

She moved as though a map was bringing her.

[POTENTIAL COUNTS FOR NOTHING UNTIL IT'S REALIZED.]

"That's Cadere's skin?"
"You recognize it?"
"No, I don't. It looks too different. The phone does."
"Hmm. How's that?"

She held her phone out and moved it across some surfaces of my body like she was testing them for toxic emissions. Near the back of my left ear lobe, she said, "Here."

"A chip?"

"I guess, but I don't know. It could be injected ink nowadays."

"Interesting. A map-point tattoo. It doesn't go 'Beep . . . . beep . . . beepbeepbeep'?"

"I can turn that on if I want."

[RECHANNELING DESTRUCTIVE IMPULSES IS A SIGN OF MATURITY.]

I invited her to sit down. It didn't feel like there was much to avoid.

[SACRIFICING YOURSELF TO A BAD CAUSE IS NOT A MORAL ACT.]

"What's in your bottle? Water?"

"Rhizome tea."

"Can I have a sip?"

She took out her thermos and unscrewed the cap. The rubber seal squeaked and the plastic clicked confidently. She turned the lid over and poured some tea in.

I took it in my hands and could feel the heat move against the skin of my fingers and extend through the flesh. My fingers and hands softened as the heat spread millimeter by millimeter across their thickness.

I raised the light green cup to my face and inhaled the smell. A dry pungency hit the insides of my nose and then tiny sparks of tickle dispersed deeper and deeper inside the sinus space of my head, stirring a sneeze to almost spasm.

My facial muscles tensed and gripped, altering the flow of space within my head. The sneeze paused and then decayed.

I sipped.

The cup had become too hot to hold, so I held it along its lip and then set it down on the arm of the chair.

[SLIPPING INTO MADNESS IS GOOD FOR THE SAKE OF COMPARISON.]

She took the cup of tea and poured what remained back in her thermos. That seemed like a mysterious act, but she did it more naturally than anything else I'd seen her do so far. It felt like a glimpse into her heart.

"Are there many others around here?"

"Others of you or me?"

"Mes, I guess. Any other beeping skins on your map?"

"I can't say."

"Because I'm not allowed to know or you don't know?"

"A bit of both. My phone can only trace you. That's all I paid for."

"Are there others with your app?"

"Following you?"

"Huh. I hadn't thought about that. But, sure."

"Probably.

"Why are you following me?"

"I have an interest that pre-dates you."

"An intimate interest?"

"Very."

"Cadere was your lover?"

"I never met him."

"Someone else had this skin?"

"That's closer."

"How much closer?"

"Much closer to me."

"Was this your skin?"

"For a good while. Maybe three years ago."

"I see. So, what do you want from me?"

She turned the cap back on the thermos. It again sang with its odd confidence.

"Can I interest you in sex?"

[STASIS IS A DREAM STATE.]

43

The city is a tool, a human tool. It is designed to fit human dimensions, from curb heights, to street lines, to walkway widths, to bridge stairs.

The walls of the city are smooth so as to not injure people with pokey protrusions. The road is flat so as to not twist a human ankle or trip one of us up. The fences are too high for us to get over. The doors let us fit through. The lights come on for our eyes to see. The benches come up to the place where our legs bend.

The city is a tool designed to help humans live. The city speaks our ideas back to us. It speaks our self-love back to us. The city lets us see ourselves as the center of intention.

The city is our mirror of celebrity.

The city is made for human purposes. It is made by and for human beings. The city is arranged on an assumption of human vision, built from and for our perspective and by the way we read spaces. It has human pace and human needs for predictability.

The city suppresses surprise.

The city is a social tool that humans live within and through and as.

In contrast to the wilderness, the city is made to assist and protect humans. It is like an extension of the layers we use to protect our bodies.

Clothes, house, city.

The city is fabricated and designed for human use. To serve humans. Flat surfaces provide predictable standing and movement. The buildings don't totter for eons like boulders before crashing down to become a new arrangement of a gravity-borne landscape. The city prohibits such creative collapse.

In the wild, the environment is a dynamic and constant source of unpredictable change. Surfaces are always uneven and unstable. For people of the ancient past, any of the thousands of rocks stepped on during a walk had the potential to roll over and sprain an ankle, or break a bare toe, or tear a foot open.

Any slope could slip, and there was no lack of slopes.

Whereas the city is a place of constructed spaces and visible predictabilities, the wilderness is always an unfixed layering of closeness and intimacy.

The wild pushes up against.

The wild pokes into.

The wild is always pressing right up to the place, moment and context of the body in it.

The city lays back.

The city is a place of visible distances. It's designed for letting a human watch the future approach. In the city, the human can always see itself, its ideas. In the city, the human stands at the center, separate and able to watch the world approach with requisite announcements of what will come.

The city comes by invitation only.

But, the wild is immediate nearness, too close to be seen. Un-apart. The wild is body intimate, invisible in its infinite hidden surfaces—any of which can erupt and trigger ripples of change. The wild is alive with open agents of collapse, independent forces that are not functioning within a system. Free agents. The wild does not follow a plan designed for, as or against anything. In the wild, humans can only try to survive amidst innumerable incidental effects.

The wild has no rule and no center. The wild is not trying to help human beings or anything else. The wild has no hope for or against. The wild can't even be called a thing because the word "thing" implies an organized entity. A part of. A structured object with recognized limits and edges. A role being played.

The wild denies organization.

In contrast, the city is a human life support system, a machine made for facilitating certain human ideas about human life. A predictable and ordered life. A rational and stable life. A delimited and clarified life. Safety centered. Responsible. Life in which you can expect to see what will come next.

As well, the city is a surface of secrets. The city's surfaces hide and protect systems that keep its human purposes going and in tune. The city's surfaces are also there to keep us from fucking up the system that maintains us. To protect us from us. There are tubes and wires and hoses and pipes that we know we'd damage if we could. We'd climb on them or swing from them or bend them or hit them with rocks just to hear them clang and explode.

We are the wild in the city. The city is there to protect us from us. To tame us.

The city knows we can't be trusted with self-perpetuation. The city knows we will destroy ourselves. That maybe we want to. Maybe we need to. Like some robot of service that runs on a code of doing no human harm, a distrust of us is part of the city's design and purpose to keep us safe, even from ourselves.

The city's surfaces hint at these hidden secrets, these markers of the city's distrust.

We can see them everywhere and speculate on their use. Locks on doors. Welds on grates. Bolts on access panels. All these barriers whisper of systems unseen. They hint at functions that are safer to keep invisible lest those the city protects let their curiosity go wild. Because, while some may refer to the unseen infrastructure of substreet tunnels, electrical hub-holes, sewer sluices, cable tracks, drainage conduits, gas piping and water ducts as an urban jungle, in fact it is the opposite. These hidden spaces are an experts-only world, requiring licenses and special passes to access.

There are no keys needed for getting into the wild.

44

On top of me, she lunged and adjusted her placement. Her rhythms, paces and angles. A self-consuming focus. An internality.

Her shoulders were backed by the shadowed ceiling. Her uncapped hair. No self-shading glasses. She was taking each moment like a grape. Singular and unique. Then, moving for a next.

Her skin was well fitted and darkened in spots. Tattoos crossing tattoos and other stains texturing her shadowed curves. Beneath her breasts. Her neck. Under arms.

I watched her body at foreshortened angles in low light with occupied attention.

She moved as an exclusive sound.

I was within her, but I knew it was her within her for her. She was having a sort of out of body experience. She was me. She was fitting into herself. Fulfilling herself in a way that seemed to reunite a semblance of the split UrHuman that Plato (was it Plato?) spoke of.

Healed.

Self-inflicted divisions rejoined.

My experience was more at a distance, or at various distances. There was no way I could fathom the intimacies she was enacting. She had been me longer than me. She was embodying dreams long stored. Dreams stirred and ranked on a spectrum of impossibles.

The body I occupied exhibited a level of affinity that I have never experienced again in it. That body longed for her. That body's memories triggered neurochemicals to rain down like a cataract accumulated in a billion tiny clouds.

There were senses igniting across the body's surface, and I could merely try to witness. I wasn't a first-degree participant. I was a necessary lurker.

Her bodies were within an electric static of secrets being flashed and answered.

Long lost lovers' code.

A storm of real.

There was no hurry after.

We slept and woke and touched and spoke. The light barely shaped the room. We were more of a tangle of darknesses than of clarity.

I leaned up and looked at her.

I would not be able to recognize her if I were to see her again. That room's dimness took her image with it.

She touched the edge of my left side, letting her finger ride the line of a scar I didn't know I had.

She said, "I got that climbing over a fallen tree. A stray wire was tangled on the log and gave me a deep scratch, and it then got infected."

"Where?"

"Hiking along a canal in Venice."

"Italy?"

"No. LA."

"Before, you said you didn't recognize Cadere."

"I never saw him. I mean, just in pictures. You know, the face is so different now. It's not what I remember. Of course, my skull is smaller than yours. And I mostly saw the face in mirrors. It didn't photograph well on me."

I looked at her folded amidst the sheets. Her hip was decorated with two patterns of contrasting lines.

"Is this your original skin?"

"No. I've lost track of that. This is a friend's."

"Are these her tattoos?"

"About half. I did most of them for her. When she died, I wanted to let them and her continue. The others were done by another friend."

She pointed at an abstract blot of black color near her ribs. She talked about having that piece done. She said that the pain was the purpose, to mark that space of the skin with a depth of pain. That fused the skin to what was beneath and before it.

The tattoo's oblong shape crossed through and mostly blacked out an earlier tattoo of an industrial bridge in the Port of Los Angeles. A place of significance for her friend, but she didn't know why. Some secret or a source of an origin.

The lack of knowledge about the story was part of the story, she said. The blotting out with pain was also part.

"Are you from Los Angeles?"

"No. Just there in Cadere's skin." She pointed at the bridge, "I met her in Shanghai. She was maybe from LA, but not in this skin. The bridge is a link to LA, but she never went back. Moved. Elsewhere."

There was a sound from somewhere outside the room. Some whirl of a motor inside of a machine.

"Do you know, Cadere isn't dead?"

"I thought he was."

"No, I hear he's not. And he's looking to get his skin back. He's been trying for a long time. When I was in it, too. That's what I was told. That's part of why I changed out."

"To this one?"

"No, one other before this. A Welsh psychogeographer."

"Kind of related."

"True."

45

Before departing from the former inhabitant of Cadere, I asked her to delete me from her tracking app.

I didn't mind her being out there and moving around in the city, but I just didn't want to think of her following me on a screen, watching me move from place to place as a blinking dot across a glass rectangle in her hand. I felt that would add an unwelcome bit of knowledge to my cache of paranoia treasure.

While, of course, I knew she could easily just resubscribe to put me back on her hunt-list, I at least wanted the space for a psychic head start.

The most exhausting aspect of the world of digital machines is that they never rest. They watch over us with the same sort of relentless concentration as a possessive lover or a possessed evangelist.

Thankfully, she agreed and I watched as she swept the icon of her locating software into the icon of her phone's trashcan.

Back out on the street, we stood next to the building where she somehow had access to the room we used. We talked about nothing while slowly moving, and then found ourselves between the Toray building and its neighbor.

Waving "Bye bye," we parted.

She walked north and I south.

She turned west, so I east.

Strangers again, passing on opposite sides of skyscrapers.

46

Proceeding down the street, I decided to start criss-crossing Nakanoshima Island.

It may have been an instinctive avoidance technique, I don't know. But my sudden plan was to just move back and forth over the island.

Then I thought I'd also try to cross all the bridges which provide access and exit to Nakanoshima.

Comings and goings.

Entrances and departures.

Presences and absences.

Because I was already midway down the length of the island, I thought it could be an interesting way to walk for however much longer I ended up going on that day.

The plan felt right and had the kind of themes I liked considering: Post-structural nomadism. Porous borders. Drift. Blurring arrivals and departures.

I didn't have any particular goal or destination. I wasn't on the streets for any logical reason any longer. I wasn't working out any certain answer to any special question. I already had my stock of drugs and I was just letting them work their effects. I didn't need a place to go for that. I didn't know if they would do what I hoped, or if they already had.

Hopefully the drugs would bring me and the Cadere skin into tune. But how could I measure if that actually occurred?

In the meanwhile, until I knew or just stopped caring, I decided to keep moving, both physically and mentally. So, I just walked.

Criss-crossing the island felt like an acceptable next stage in my day.

47

After consciously starting, I quickly had the feeling that bridges were an important thing to think about. It could have been an after-effect from a cloudy capsule of cough medicine, or the disembodied sex, but I had a strong feeling that bridges were things I could learn from.

Within a few steps of that consideration, the memory of being with the former-Cadere woman flashed back into my mind and it entangled itself in my initial thoughts of bridges.

Her body. My body. This body.

I formed a link—in whatever way links form—and from it a line of thought blossomed as some voice lecturing in my brain. This sentence appeared: "Bridges and skins facilitate meeting embodiments." Within a few more steps, that rather poetic sentence was edited to: "Like bridges, skins embody meetings."

When that line and its revision came up, the idea seemed both elusive and probing. Insightful and bullshit.

Maybe you feel something similar.

I didn't know what it meant, but I felt it had something interesting. It was going somewhere.

And, as I walked, thoughts started flowing to explore the dim interior of that idea. My thoughts searched the idea's dimensions and structure for light switches or a TV set.

Did the idea have legs to run on, or stumble, or crawl? Or was it born crippled? Anyway it could, I felt the idea would move. It would go somewhere. It would take my mind somewhere.

So, as I drifted down the street, around a corner, across an intersection and over a bridge, tendrils of reasoning for the idea began to assemble. They dimly revealed and furnished the idea's initially vacant space.

This is an interesting thing about walking self-talk. The pace of walking feels somehow fitting for thought. The flow and the shifts and the step-by-step arrivals into new yet slightly familiarly unfamiliar surroundings make thoughts attract other thoughts and assemble into an understanding.

As I walked, ideas tangled and revised themselves. A sense for making sense from nothing came into play and the ideas found forms, tested weaknesses, explored assumptions and edited logics.

The whole while walking, the thought-talk pulled ideas out of what was at hand around me as my body moved through the streets. My mind incorporated scattered and random details of the world and sometimes adopted them as metaphors for conveying the abstract, for making a sense make sense.

I walked and my minds talked.

Feel free to jump forward to the next chapter, but this is the lecture they said:

ViaMeters: Of Embodiments

Bridges and skins have a distinct non-ness. Rather than being autonomous, they each serve to connect an existent entity with its assumed wholeness, with its more complete expanse, with its fullness and presence. Bridges and skins cause continuity. The bridge connects some piece of land to another piece of land, linking them as a larger expanse of territory. Likewise, the skin connects the slippery and fragmented moments of self to itself as a continuous state, or maybe even—as some say—to its eternal life. The big wholes. Land flows in space via bridges. Self flows in time through bodies. And both bridges and skins serve as traces of distinctions in the wholes of either land or self. Bridges and skins are absences where a whole meets the rest of its whole, more of its wholeness. Gaps (either in space or time), a bridge and a skin exist as a vivid not-ness, an absence of place or an absence of time relative to the whole, relative to the land or self. The bridge is a not here and not there, serving as a passageway to unify location. A bridge is a suspension of place that lets place become, or complete, place. Likewise, the skin is not this and not that, but rather a means for the self to alter and maintain unity through time. The body is constantly undergoing momentary transitional states of absence via which self maintains self.

As the skin-enwrapped body is not what the self ever associates itself with or reduces itself to, the body is the means by which self endures and becomes. The self becomes its whole or full self via the body. The body—like a bridge—is considered to be primarily a functional, if temporal, object. It is a thing doing various lesser things that are determined by certain limits of purpose. The body breathes, digests, moves, eats, lives, etc. All to keep the continuity of the self intact. To keep self going. To keep me alive. The body isn't allowed to speak with a voice of its own. Or the degree to which the body speaks is not considered worth much, not valuable, not valid, not heard. The body speaks but is not understood. The tongue is thought to only speak for the self. What would the tongue say for itself? The body isn't considered autonomous or given any independence even though it ceaselessly does its life-sustaining tasks on its own. In fact, the tongue never stops speaking. But the self doesn't much care. The body dutifully fulfills the tasks which the self assumes are the body's purpose, but the self doesn't really have any understanding of how the body does this stuff. The self is busily consumed with being self while the body is supposed to dumbly and mutely work on keeping the seamlessness of self proceeding without interruption. The body is to keep time going for the self's selfish consideration of self. The body is the self's ephemeral time machine, a device used to keep the self existing, either from moment to moment or through life after life. Useful, but ultimately disposable. Mortal.

Similarly, the land is considered to be the stable condition, the location, the place, the shape of what is, the terra firma definitive. Land is named, fought for, taken, occupied, dug, shaped and bordered. While rivers might be used as the semi-invisible lines that end and start and define the contours of the land, it is the land that is the united depth, the everlasting. Under every river— and even beneath the ocean—is land. The continuity of the whole. Rivers are temporal, their fluid-flexible flow an embodiment of change. You can never enter the same river twice. Bridges are even more temporary and without self-existence. They serve to unite the land with the land and by extension make the land's apparent stability consistent and secure. Bridges extend across voids and over states of fluidity that are to be ignored. Bridges make the idea of stability itself absolute.

Bridges and bodies function as tools to perpetuate land and self, to keep the assumed firmness, stability and unity of land and self uninterrupted. To connect land to land and self with self. Via bridges and bodies, the goals of these larger contextualizing expanses—these valued entities, these wholenesses of worth—can be perpetuated. Via bridges and bodies, these expanses are located and calendared.

But, also, bridges and bodies serve as traces of an inherent instability within these speculated vastnesses. As traces, they indicate that space and time require Vehicles of Via, linking logics of nowhere and nowhen in order to assemble particle fragments into wholes and to nullify the radically explosive powers of nows and emptinesses. Or rather, we as thinking beings need space and time to seem to be connected structures and stable wholes. Without such connective logics, important structures that make self-construction possible would be lacking. We need narrative glues and other joining screws. So, in these ways, bridges and bodies work like ViaMeters: indicators of methods at work in between, means which are used to form connected wholes via mediums that otherwise don't exist. Wholes are constructs and we are their builders. Or, rather, wholes exist in such limited and purpose-bound ways that they don't have their own autonomy. ViaMeters exist to serve the whole, or to imply there is a larger state of completeness which is then considered to be of more real value or to have more genuine permanence. ViaMeters are the traces of seams in the assumed uniform hierarchy of being.

A bridge gives a sense of continuity to otherwise disparate spaces. As we walk or drive on a surface of land, we don't feel obstructed if we can access a bridge and keep our flowing going. At such times, the river or whatever divides seems to vanish from value. Likewise, a body keeps a series of selves intact, providing continuity for what would otherwise be a chaos of lost voices or a disjointed plurality of brevities. The physical consistency of the body lets the self continue though time, and to also keep track of time. It gives a sense of an ongoing. The body doesn't forget time. It becomes the self's vehicle of memory. The body is the self's reminder. Its remainer. All the body's physicality is marked with links between real pasts and real presents. The body orients a continuity to events beyond self, to elements which link self to self. For example, my left hand has continued to be attached here at my wrist since yesterday and/or 10 years ago, and/or since birth.

Regardless of how my self might envision itself as an abstraction, it recognizes itself as connected to itself via reference to my left hand's continuity. My self relocates itself as self via my left hand because the hand is consistently there and recognized because it's always there. Even if the self stops paying attention to the hand, the hand maintains a memorable consistency of location, and via that connection, the self re-assumes itself to be consistent due to its association to the hand. And this is equally true with the rest of my body and the physical world I recognize as being mine. In this way, the world becomes my extended body. My selfish world. I recognize my self's consistency through everything, again and again. The bodyworld consistency constantly reorients me as being a continuous self, repeatedly associating myself to self via such apparently continuing objects.

For example, yesterday I accidentally hit a knuckle on my left hand with a red pen. The mark remains today and this small temporary squiggle of red ink serves as a trace of my self. It connects me to that moment yesterday when the narrative mark happened on my knuckle. Without such traces, self would drift, flicker and dissolve. These details serve as ViaMeters. There is also a scar on my right middle finger that has been there for as long as I can remember, but now it surprises me when I look for it and I realize Cadere's skin doesn't have it. A sudden suspension of continuity occurs which I can only make sense of by remembering that this has not been my only skin. Some other skin is moving around with that little scar, or perhaps it is folded in a box in a closet somewhere. But, oddly, I still feel a unity with it. I feel a me-ness through it, some expansion of affinity fragments. I still feel that little middle-finger scar belongs to me, or I belong to myself through it. How long I will feel this affinity to it, I don't know. Maybe that's what today's drugs are for. These intimacies of continuity—details that are ephemeral and enduring and absent—serve to connect the self to the self, letting the self assume continuation. The body provides the self with a mode of keeping track of being. All that would otherwise evaporate as ephemeral as fog. The body serves as a memory-marker in time that enables the self to reference and recite its narrative back through all that has been its previous, and into what new traces connect to its nexts. The body is the undeniable and trusted object that stores the self's culminating transitions through transience. The body is the assembled mark of reference. The body is the self's overlay of moment and memory. The body reassures the self's assumption of unity.

48

A stainless-steel container truck made a clanging empty rumble as it moved across the sky.

When I came out of my revelry of internal discourses about bridges and bodies, I found myself standing on the Nishikibashi bridge. I was looking up at a distance.

Trance-like and dazzled.

How did I get here?

My eyes were calmly fixed on the span of a suspended highway which snakes its way between some of the canyons created by Osaka's densely clustered districts of office buildings.

The delivery truck's shining silver box smoothly moved north, 30-or-so meters above the Tosabori River's fluid grey-green surface.

I looked around at where I was standing. It took a few moments to reassemble the steps of how I'd gotten to that spot on that bridge. In the process of walking, I must have gone south over Higobashi bridge and then crossed Yotsubashisuji Boulevard at the signal, but I had only vague recollections of the pieces of that stroll.

I was seemingly on auto-pilot. My body was doing its independent duty as my mind wandered amidst ideas. My body was taking care of itself in the world while my mind was off in LectureLand.

But yet I had memory-snippets of a woman's yellow handbag, a black rubber seam inset in the road's surface, the glint of the sun off a piece of traffic equipment and the repeating ping-poog pattern of the crosswalk's sound-signal for blind pedestrians.

All these traces linked me from where I was standing on Nishikibashi bridge to a series of other places through space. I came here from way over there at where my thinking started. Where I was from where I was.

Standing at the top of the bridge's cold stone steps, I took out my phone and typed in some notes to store the couple hundred meters of thinking I'd gone through on my way to that spot on the bridge. My notes on my progress through "ViaMeters."

How long I'd been standing there on the bridge was hard to say. Surely not long, but it felt like I'd entered a different time and place. I'd come out of something and into something else. Through a threshold of contemplation.

My knees kind of ached from standing on that cold stone bridge for however long.

Once the concept of ViaMeters came into focus, and then the word for it appeared, it was hard for me to not see ViaMeters everywhere. (Isn't that the way it is with ideas and the words that give them form and limit?) For me, ViaMeters are the immeasurable non-entities that facilitate connections of spaces and durations of time in everything. They are the means by which we leap or gloss over fragmenting seams in order to sense whatever we sense as continuity. They are the aspects that can be or must be overlooked, ignored or subsumed for the construction of stable and complete forms.

Sacrificial lacks.

ViaMeters are a speculative measure of conduiticity.

And, while they make sense to me, I will probably never consciously think about them again. They seem to lack some ease of explication that useful ideas need in order to spread or stay current.

ViaMeters are likely just the ephemeral fruits of a stroll.

49

After finishing my notes, I stood there, just looking around. I touched the skin behind my left ear. I felt like I had felt a warm pulse beneath the skin, and so touched there to check. I wondered if it was my blood throbbing or if someone's app was now trained on me again.

I wandered around the place where I was on the bridge.

Then, I noticed that Nishikibashi Bridge was home to a small visual history of bridges. Osaka city had installed a permanent display of weather-proof images showing famous bridges from the city's past.

For as long as could be called forever, Osaka has been a city of flowing waters.

In a prehistoric time before the city got the name Osaka (meaning Big Slope), the area's geography consisted of a hill overlooking an inland sea. In that time when the water level was up to where fourth-floor windows open now, there were whales and other monsters of the liquidinous shifts plying the spaces of what now is city. Fish were swimming where now only sparrows and crows fly.

In an area which is now just east of the city's treeless concrete sprawl, ocean waves once broke against cliffs.

That north/south cliff line is where the Tanimachi subway now runs, but then it was the foot of the city's namesake big slope.

Eventually, as the waters dropped, this western-facing 200-meter rise became home to the area's early Buddhist temples. The sun setting in the west is the reference point for the distant

Pure Land of Amida Buddha. So, the temples were placed on the western slope and the sun was used as the star upon which temple builders aligned their entrance gates, prayer hall layouts and the gazes of serene-faced statues.

For centuries before those medieval Buddhist buildings appeared, the evening view from the hill was just of the sun setting into a vast body of water. But as the sea gradually receded, hundreds of island protrusions began to arise and darkly dot the basin's expansive liquid gloss.

We can imagine ourselves standing on the Uemachi Plateau 1,000 years ago and seeing a vast delta fed by the Yodogawa river. At sunset, spits of silt draw long black lines onto the shimmering water. As well, the revealed peaks of many low-floating islands must have dotted the gloss as shadowy black oblongs.

The city in its current form is a flattened encasement of concrete, but it still maintains echoes of those many islands. In names. Hundreds of neighborhoods and block-clusters across the urban core whisper of locations where once were islands: Fukushima, Dojima, Chushojima, Shikanjima, Miyakojima, Kunijima, Sakurajima, Maishima, Enokojima, Chishima, Ikejima, Torishima, Nishinakajima, Kitaokajima, etc.

And, over the centuries, as more of the islands became low-rise hills linked by swamp-muck and muddy silt, people began wading down from the big slope. They descended and tested the gummy land for its potential stabilities.

Where would a stick stand?

Where could rocks be piled into walls?

Where could drainage be channeled to keep a pathway or bedroom dry?

Where a hut? Where a shop? Where a house? Where a shrine?

For generations, Osakans shaped the soil. They moved the earth and gave birth to rivers.

Sea waters gradually became secluded into Osaka Bay. The ocean was pushed out by the pressures fed by fresh water flowing in via the Yodogawa River.

The ocean was also stored in ice.

The river's delta expanded and the sea gave way to the new. To human inhabitation. To a city called Osaka. To the pressures of human ideas, plans and methods.

The liquid world was transformed into municipal earth by Osaka's powerful warlords and visionary patrons.

Human-designed lines were put into action by Hideyoshi and Ieyasu.

The love of rational straight edges and right-angled corners is visible everywhere now.

The flows of waters were channeled and curbed into directions by the sounds of sticks scrapping dirt into embankments. Tooling the land to make it human. Plans were enacted. Osaka's soil was dug, moved, filled, piled, packed, reinforced, reimagined and mapped.

Island lumps in the landscape melted as their soil was broken, lifted, spread and linked with other extinct islands to form what maps from the 1800s show to be a city of roughly 20 major island divisions that are squared-off and interlaced by a grid system of north/south east/west canals.

As the islands and hills flattened into broad square bodies edged by embankments, the rivers flowed between. The water ran through canals and other boulevards of boat traffic. And thus, as the city settled more and more into being a center of trades and merchants and populations, the city's different island districts became connected together via the birth of seemingly too many bridges to count.

The ancient mythogeography of Japan famously said that there were 8,008 temples in Kyoto. With similar ideals, Osaka was called a city of 8,008 bridges.

Drawing on the way the Kanji character for "8" [八] appears to reach down while opening out expansively—expanding out to indicate an infinite vastness—the number 8,008 was an auspicious way to imply incredible abundance.

And while official estimates say that Osaka actually had only about 2,000 bridges, this number probably doesn't include the innumerable unofficial, unnamed and unmapped ad-hoc bridges, zigzagging plank assemblages and other make-do dry passageways set up over sewers and other bodies of muck that neighborhood residents surely used to safely move from solid to solid.

We can surely find a way to count an auspicious 8,008 bridges in Osaka.

Osaka doesn't still have 2000 bridges. But it has many.

And, while a lot of its old bridges (or *bashi*) are gone, place names like Shinsaibashi, Nagahoribashi, Chidoribashi, Yotsubashi, Nishiohashi, Imabashi, Tenjinbashi, Funahashi, Nipponbashi, Watanabebashi, Sakurabashi, Temmabashi, Kyobashi, Tsuruhashi, Oebashi, and many more maintain the memory of the once abundant existence of bridges.

That said, Osaka is still home to a large number of bridges. There are bridges of stone, concrete, metal, wood and rope. There is even an underwater "bridge" via which pedestrians and bicyclists can pass beneath the Ajigawa river.

I am sure there must be a bridge made of glass somewhere in the city, but I've not found it yet. It just seems necessary. And, while a paper bridge might seem to be pushing the impractical too far, I have my hope that the architect Shigeru Ban might land a commission someday, even if just for a temporary bridge of cardboard as part of some exhibition of experimental paper technology.

50

A catch started as I was passing behind Festival Hall.

I doubted its real importance from right off, but I couldn't stop feeling it.

Midway down the back of my right calf, between the Cadere skin and the meat that was mine.

A catch.

At first it was like a very tiny hook, barely felt but definitely felt. Like the smallest roughness on a fingernail when moving across a blanket. Causing nothing to really stop, but marking the movement with a moment caught in the progress. A snag in a smooth flow.

I continued walking. Forgetting it.

Then, it happened again.

And again at what started to become an almost predictable pace. Evidence of a mechanism at work. Cause and effect.

Every four steps.

Then every six and a half.

No sign of trouble or pain.

Just a regular snip. A little hook. A tiny catch.

I scratched the skin on my right leg, trying to make whatever was inside shift into insensible. To break up whatever system had become set up.

No difference.

Seven steps. Catch. Seven steps. Catch.

Nine steps. Catch.

Then, seven steps again before the catch. Same place.

Then, almost the same place. Just to the outer side of the center line midway between my calf and heel.

I rubbed the top of my left shoe against it, as if polishing my shoe's top surface.

No change.

But, maybe it went straight center? Not one side or the other, just center.

Maybe.

I paid attention until I noticed I wasn't noticing anymore.

Then I was, but the catch seemed to have moved to just inside the center line, but was happening every other right step. How long had that been like that?

I passed beneath the span of the overhead highway.

I rubbed the spot again, and then it was gone for three steps.

Then it was back at the center again, but also another catch appeared farther up on the calve, outside of the center line.

Two catches.

They'd switch back and forth every other step of my right foot.

Two steps upper.

Two steps lower. For maybe 5 minutes of walking this went on.

Then, suddenly, "Ouch!"

The lower one bit like an insect inside the skin.

I stooped down and massaged the area with my thumbs, trying to just scramble whatever mysterious system was setting itself up in there, in the space between me and the skin.

What was actually happening in there didn't matter to me, as long as it stopped.

I could imagine an infinite number of possible fictions, but each of them was no more or less relevant than the single unknown fact that had become engaged at that time. Its ability to arise just one time, to set up a noticeable existence as its own and then vanish made it an eventful phenomenon. It was something that made me question whether I was merely existing for this catch's expression at that time.

It even made me question whether its non-noticeable condition was equal to—or exceeded—the duration of its catching.

51

I was never able to tell for sure what had caused that catching in my calf, but when I removed the Cadere skin a few weeks later, I found a single red hair high up on my right thigh muscle. It was wound into a twisted tangle.

I carefully untangled it and checked its length against the two points where I remembered sensing the catchings were happening on my right calve. The hair was too short to reach both places—which doesn't necessarily prove anything.

I have no idea where the red hair could have come from. I know no one with red hair, and in Japan red hair is rare. I can't think of any red-haired person ever being in my apartment, let alone the room where I change skins.

Perhaps the hair had fallen into the skin when it was packed up. Or, from when the skin was removed by Cadere, or from the people between him and me. Or, it could have stowed itself away between fibers of my muscles long ago, smuggled into contact with my flesh via some other skin I wore years ago. It could have been on any of the many floors I have laid down on while skinless.

The enduring existence of a single red hair means it has held a place at every moment of its existence, regardless of my inability to track it.

Everything has to be somewhere.

Existence proves history.

52

Writing and wandering in 18th-century Osaka, the mendicant Zen monk Ryokyu lived an overlay of body and abode. Ryokyu was a calligraphist poet of an idiosyncratic form of brush writing.

He didn't use black *sumi* ink directly. He dipped his brush in water and then wrote on small squares of *washi* paper.

Using water with a single continuous flow of stroke, he'd write *kanji* characters that often didn't exist within the typical Japanese character forms. He called these characters, "allusional *kanji*." And sometimes he called them, "ghosts." Because, as he explained, "ghosts are struggling between what they were and something else, what they assume to know and don't."

Ryokyu's ghost characters were unique calligraphic forms inspired by formal, meaning-bound *kanji*. He tweaked the formal into becoming hybrids of private instincts.

He seemed to know the meanings for these ghost *kanji* he created, but perhaps only temporarily.

Regardless of whether he knew the meanings or not, he never translated them into standard Japanese or explained their unique nuances. So, most all of their meaning potential is lost.

Ryokyu loved and distrusted language, using it as more of an armature of senses, both the fleeting and the patterned.

His time in meditation had shown him how language can't help but be indirect, and so he used language in ways that both visibly and symbolically dissolved as well as involved beyond his intentions.

Rather than set a meaning too firmly and confidently in place, Ryokyu wanted language which would forget itself, hint like dreams, evaporate and fade like a scent. He wanted language which absorbed and released more than was in his control. For him, meaning was not particularly important or valuable. Rather, the moment of of, when a meaning congeals into its brief shimmer, is what he hoped to source or refer to. He wanted to hint at that dynamic of life/sense/understanding that is coming together in the same momentary phase as it falls apart.

Thus, the way he wrote his poetry involved these concerns.

Using water, Ryokyu would write one of his allusional *kanji* characters, or "ghosts," on paper. Once the character was present, he'd blow a fine dust of charcoal over the wet surface. The black dust adhered to the damp-but-drying shapes of allusional language. Once dry, he'd hold the paper up and tap against it to let the powder that didn't stick fall back into his "dust box."

Then he'd write the next character over the top of the previous on the same sheet of paper.

In this way, Ryokyu would amass a composition which both obscured and entangled itself, blurred and augmented itself, messied and revealed itself beyond the stability of plotting and design and knowing.

Collaborative slurry words.

Fire dust mud.

Thoughts unthought.

One theme that Ryokyu explored repeatedly was the abode-body, or the body as place of living. Again and again, he examined the structures within which life lives, the occupied residences and ephemeral contours of pulsing meat walls. At least 25 of Ryokyu's extant paintings/poems deal with overlaying "ghosts" that are derived from words for "abode," "house," "body," "flesh," "dwell," "occupy," etc.

None of these pieces strictly maintain those terms by sticking to their *kanji* forms. Rather, as his brother quoted Ryokyu saying, the ghosts' "echoes seem to ring from hammers on those bells." These paintings/poems by Ryokyu involve allusively sounding these concepts.

And, to be clear, Ryokyu's brother is how we know everything we know about Ryokyu's approach to painting/poetry and any methods for how to decipher his poems/paintings.

Everything we know is from Ryokyu's elder brother, Go Shida.

Shida raised Ryokyu. And Ryokyu would return to see him as part of his circuits of ritual *takuhatsu* begging.

Shida was a sandal maker with an active workshop in a central district of Osaka, near what is now Hommachi. Providing a number of designs to Osaka's clothing merchants, his most enduring sandal design used *tatami* mat as the foot bed. This design was adopted and adapted by many other makers and still continues to be a common style in today's Japanese sandal industry.

Shida kept journals and notes documenting his daily activities, sandal designs, local happenings, foods eaten and of

Ryokyu's visits. This is how we know about Ryokyu, from him showing up at Shida's home or workshop, often times unannounced.

On occasion, Shida noted in his journal that Ryokyu had sent word that his begging route would bring him nearby at a certain time, and some of these visits are supported by entries later in Shida's journal documenting when Ryokyu had actually visited.

While Shida mostly wrote about his own daily work and personal activities, his notes regularly include his thoughts about his little brother. Through these writings, we can get hints of Ryokyu's calligraphic approaches and potential poetic goals. Or, at least to the degree that Shida understood them.

Regarding his brother, Shida writes, "Looking through his eyes, the world's separate lines are tangled," and "He says, 'If I didn't shave my head, I'd never comb my hair.'" (A "shaved head" is a symbolic image in Japanese culture for a Buddhist monk, while "uncombed hair" symbolizes madness).

In a rather long entry made after a year of no contact from Ryokyu—a time during which Shida had worried that his brother might have died somewhere on the road and that he might never learn word of his demise—Shida writes that Ryokyu appeared at his door like a "spring bird dropped from a winter cloud," full of unexpected energy. Shida notes that Ryokyu's monk's shoulder sack was thick with poems, or "dust pages," as Shida referred to them.

Shida gave Ryokyu a hearty welcome and Ryokyu stayed with him for close to a week, partly to nurse an injured ankle. Shida wrote that Ryokyu was animated and vibrant in talking with his big brother. Shida felt his brother had returned from the dead and the vivid feeling of how easily life could vanish made him eager to know about Ryokyu's obvious passion for making his painted slips of paper.

Shida documents that he asked Ryokyu many questions, probing for understanding to the artwork. In these exchanges, Shida learned about Ryokyu's method of painting and was able to have Ryokyu point out how he "reads" his "collapsed poems."

Ryokyu calls them "collapsed poems" only in that exchange, and Shida comments that this was a term he'd never heard before.

Shida writes that Ryokyu explained that the stroked lines of meaning fall on top of each other like how the moments of life leave the past and present always roiling together. While this is the only time the term, "collapsed poems" is used, the explanation is particularly illuminating.

53

My introduction of Ryokyu above has a purpose. It is so that I can now talk about a failure that Ryokyu's work inspired.

Not Ryokyu's failure.

Rather, a failing piece of public sculpture that was installed on the Nakanoshima Garden Bridge spanning the Dojima river just west of Yodoyabashi.

The connection between the sculpture and Ryokyu is merely that Ryokyu was enjoying a brief period of public popularity in the 1980s. This was when NHK Television Osaka produced a well-rated documentary about him and his brother. The program was drawn from and dramatized Shida's journals.

Partly due to this show's popularity, the artist who won the public sculpture commission referenced Ryokyu as an inspiration for his proposed work's concept.

The work was accepted and granted its present place on Nakanoshima Garden Bridge. Unfortunately, the work is obviously burdened with the tedious hallmarks of municipally commissioned sculpture: work that is publicly funded and over-directed by city officials.

Close to five meters tall, the sculpture consists of a round concrete base supporting the outlines of four human forms that are joined at—or are appearing from—a common center-point.

The two female and two male forms extend out from their shared source and take up four different poses, as if in a dance of emergence. Each human is represented in outline form by a thick greenish "line" of bronze. The female forms are distinguished from the males by having a flair of hair. Not by breasts. Not by penises.

All the forms are empty inside and seemingly nude.

The work reeks of obvious efforts to not offend and to avoid challenging expectations too much. There are dynamics and degrees of abstraction in the piece, but viewers never have to fear that any leap into too vast (or too dark) a void might be required on their part. Reassuring and safe meanings are easily accessible on the surface of the work.

A man reaches out for something.

A woman waves at something.

A man crouches to touch something.

A woman welcomes something.

Each posturing outline hints at a gesture, and through each gesture the artwork provides an easy-to-assume narrative which can fit the action that is outlined by bronze, and thereby the work reassures the viewer that meaning is easy to secure, and that that secure meaning comfortably reinforces familiar structures about social behavior, gender, effort, purpose, being in the world, etc. Don't fret, you won't be asked to wonder.

The work offers empty human husks which viewers can slip themselves into and thereby fulfill their expected or assigned roles through.

Form determines function.

The man reaches to attain his ambitious aims.

The woman embodies friendship.

The man bends down to teach the future's children.

The woman embodies welcome and hospitality.

Such readings can be accessed in a glance and so the artwork demands no further time spent in contemplation by a passing pedestrian. No need to pause. No need to question or reflect.

The bronze work rubber-stamps assumptions and doesn't problematize meaning-making.

The work says, life is a dance of fulfilling programmed behaviors.

The viewer can feel self-approved and then proceed on to his or her own day of scripted life gestures.

This kind of work gives lazy viewers many easy escape hatches so they can opt out of exploring darker tunnels or venturing down more confounding paths that might lead a more contemplative person-who-stares-too-long deep into an unknown territory of questions and lostness.

But, I'm just such a too-long-starer.

And I love getting lost.

So, when I came across this piece of crap sculpture on the bridge on my walk, I ended up engaging it for close to an hour.

As with much of my experience on that February day, this particular excess might be attributable to the medical cocktails I'd been consuming. But I don't think my thinking was altered or falsely engaged in any way.

You be the judge.

And, while I could objectively argue now that that sculpture doesn't deserve an hour of attention, it did serve to give me access to some insights that I find of interest, and which do seem to actually link to Ryokyu.

So, I'll share them here as part of my day on the streets.

54

As I said above, the lack-luster aspects of the work make it obviously hesitant and awkward. You can sense how much the artist's plan had been tweaked by committees of approval. Each person who gave his stamp to fund the work surely required some addition, subtraction, reduction or augmentation to the work. Some alternative of some material. Some increase of obviousness in aspects that had perhaps previously been subtle. Some pumping up of positive and energetic aspects. Some hyper-upbeatification.

However, even given all these burdens on the work, the sculpture also contains some secret doors that offer access into unknown territories. With some contemplative viewing, it is possible to enter the work's less obvious (or unintentional) layers. And the artwork gives some rewarding journeys for such efforts of concentrated looking.

To start with, the work's circular base implies that there is no front or authoritative way for looking at the piece. This fact opens the piece up to change and chance. The sculpture welcomes viewing it in continuous motion by circumambulating the forms. Movement gives the piece a new dynamic life. A viewer's engaged action sets the piece into motion.

Through such an orbiting perspective, the piece becomes lighter. The previously heavy, bent metal lines which dutifully form the purposeful roles of human bodies suddenly become active and ever-altering. In motion, the bronze lines become slices of time. The shifting lines become samples of moments cut from dimensions that exceed them. In the moving eye, the sculpture's cross-sectional lines become kinetic with growth and retraction, foreshortening and reach, entanglement and shrink.

In orbit, the more obvious four viewing angles drift through each other. The predictable human forms become less human-only, transforming into knots of obscurance and otherness. For the moving viewer, new forms climb out of lostness and hint at potential forms that are lurking between forms.

Lines whisper through lines.

Meanings mumble within other meanings.

Human actions become gestures of unknown peoples, reverberating, multiplied, interactional with others.

Trans-human dance.

Pre-human sign language.

UrHuman becoming through other. Before categories of form, there may have been more mingling of plurals. The artwork hints that beings extend from others and are extensions of a sharing.

Form comes from blur, and then goes back into blur. We can glimpse learned shapes momentarily, but then things become unsure, become open, become other.

As well, as I circled and watched the piece for a longer time, my eyes started to look past the heavy, bronze humanish lines. My gaze passed through the vacant bodily forms, beyond the human gestural limits and then I saw that the sculpture's absences are filled-in with the city and the zones of sky that are beyond them.

The empty bodies become made of highways, office windows and passing birds.

Distant exteriors fill the human interiors.

Then the work seems to include me as the viewer in interesting ways. The sculptural forms become stand-ins for me. The clouds and power lines are within me. The "out there" is the "in here."

Context embodies content.

The crouch, wave, reach and welcome of the four featured figures become momentary, transitional and frail gestures trying to lay temporal borders around what exceeds and fulfills them.

Only a thin line of form divides every thing from everything. The distance from here to there, from this to that, is almost non-existent. Form is merely an ephemerally recognizable layer lost amidst the saturating thickness of everything else. And this layer-line seems to be flimsy, frightened and absurd if it is supposed to hold back the vast absolute and intensity contextualizing and imbuing formlessness.

This fragile and thin shell of us just marks one side of a core, in contrast to more and more and more core.

It's ultimately all core.

The outside reaches through and within us.

We look through form to see each other and also see the city's infrastructure.

Is there much difference? Are my thoughts much different from the cell phone tower atop the bank building? My thoughts make this. The cell phone tower is the embodied thoughts of others. Everywhere are thoughts and forms created of and by thoughts. The cell tower exists because I use it and I exist partly because I use it. I exist because it uses me.

Is this post-human communion?

And here is where I find traces of Ryokyu rising and falling through this artwork's layers and surfaces.

Rather than keeping forms sorted and separate, Ryokyu's work lets form become other and become lost. The body and the abode enjoy mutual embodiment.

The exterior and the contained collaborate.

The skin and the meat.

Everything is a part, rather than apart.

55

At some point in my hour of walking around the sculpture, I decided to take a nap, or give in to dizzy medicated urges for unconsciousness.

I sat down on the bench encircling the sculpture's base and was out quick.

When I came to, I found there was a sleeping man curled gently next to me on the cornerless bench's ledge.

Where did he come from?

Looking at the man sleeping there, I could see traces of his pasts and futures. I could see through surfaces of his present. I looked into layers of what he was and will become.

I wondered how many medicines I took were time-release.

Logical precursors and eventualities.

I looked at the man's surface and saw how other times filled his present moment. I saw linkages over time that made the now vividly evident as a crucial point for shuffling between other distinctions of time.

Was I still on my ViaMeters binge?

Moving from pasts to futures, the present is made evident as time's trajectorial tracing.

The man wore white sport shoes that were ill-fitting and obviously too big. Heavily scuffed, the energy of his walking scraped lines across the surfaces of the shoes' white rubber and leather. Lines of motion. Lines of direction. Lines of pressure, friction and thrust.

These lines were easy to read. They made it clear that he had long had trouble walking. His disability marked his shoes with the grime-packed angles of etch that his every sliding step reinforced.

He was a foot-slider.

From this hint, I noticed that the pants leg I could see was oddly wrinkled on the outside. His knees likely bent out to the sides.

The way he slept on the concrete bench hinted that he'd become used to its hard surface. He knew how the sun would shine on him at that time of day.

He was a resident here. He knew how to fit his body into this particular confluence of the world. He knew how to derive some small comfort and warmth from a hard, cold world.

A book beneath his head softened his contact with the bench. The book's blue rectangle also slightly framed the rounded edge of his face.

When he yawned, I saw the degree of tooth decay and loss.

On his ear, the scar of an old piercing.

His greying hair was wild but not evidently dirty, pushed back in a flow of active strands.

His hands were smooth, thick and burnished from exposure.

His nails, impeccably tended.

A dark brown jacket obviously encased other thick layers. It was still that time of year.

And on the ground, he'd lined up his tools. Neatly placed within reach of his sleeping body, he had a series of sacks, a metal thermos and an odd shiny object propped up inside of an open wooden box.

After a few moments of blank staring, I recognized the shiny object as a stainless-steel sextant. A black notebook cushioned the sextant's contact against the box.

As I stared at his objects, my mind flooded with speculative realities.

I imagined him sailing alone across the city in an invisible boat, or perhaps plotting points and setting out for locations without regard for terrestrial maps.

Then he spoke.

I was startled because I had assumed he was still asleep.

Obviously, he wasn't.

His voice was a gentle whisper. It reached me as a calm ripple without hint of agitation.

He referred to me as his "friend on the bench" and welcomed me to share this good place to pause. His Japanese was soft and incomplete, suspended with durations of silence but shining with curiosity.

He'd seen me looking at his sextant and other materials, and he could tell I was interested.

In a slightly singing English, he said, "My map." Then he gestured at the row of sacks standing ready within his reach.

He touched one of the bags and the plastic gave a crinkling response.

He sat up quickly and moved to show me.

He pulled a sack out from between several others and set it on the concrete ledge between us. His fingers plunged into the layers of papers and pulled out a folded bundle.

"Here," he said, as he opened the stack of pages to reveal rows after rows of numbers. Each was a penciled entry including a reading of degrees, minutes and tenths that he had evidently used his sextant to determine.

I assumed by "Here," he meant that these numbers represented where we were, maybe the particular location of the bench.

But his "here" might have held a wider scope.

I couldn't really understand how all these numbers could be used to orient us.

He maybe saw that I was puzzled looking at the data, and so he started to explain.

"These make this," he said, as he gently turned through the gathered pages and arrived at a folded sheet of larger paper set behind the collected data.

He carefully unfolded that sheet and I saw an oblong shape made up of thousands of thin pencil lines. Each line was ruler-edge straight and delicately drawn. A draftsman's hand for linearity.

From a central black dot about the size of a pupil, each grey line radiated out in a different direction. At the end of each line was a cornered bend, the angle of which was labelled with its degree. Each of the radiating lines and their bent endings was a different length, obviously indicating some specific data that didn't need to be numerically noted. At least not for him. For me, the meaning was lost.

A mystery of exactitudes.

The pencil-drawn object pulsed with dynamic energy and passionate concentration. Its lines made it glow like an echo of the sun. But, its meaning remained obscured to me.

Then, the man tried to clue me in by saying in English, "This gives me 3D."

"3D?"

That didn't help me, but I could feel the eagerness of his desire for me to get it.

56

The man wanted me to know what he knew, to share his understanding to some degree.

Then, he started to speak again and I looked up at him.

I looked at his face and noticed for the first time that he was blind in his left eye. But not simply blind. Rather, his left eye had suffered some catastrophe that had turned it into a scorched blank. His left eye was an eroded vacancy.

I clenched inside and ended up staring too long.

I could tell he could see that I was shocked at his injury. My eyes were locked on his lack.

He paused, as though he knew his voice could no longer reach through the stun. He had no way to proceed if I was going to let his blind eye make me deaf.

Difference facilitates divides.

So, as if to build a bridge, I said, "Your eye. Are you okay?"

"The Bible gave me this," he said, gesturing at what remained of his left eye.

I didn't understand what that meant at all.

But then he pointed again at the radiating pattern on the page. It was not dissimilar to the grey iris of an eye. He said, "This gives me 3D."

He grew animated. He gestured and spoke in a flow of Japanese that was beyond me.

He pointed at the tops of buildings, and then at particular grey lines extending out from the central black dot. He pointed back and forth from what surrounded us and to the dot's lines, as though weaving an invisible web of connections. He pointed his finger at a particular line on the page and then pointed to a particular office building's peak. Then he slowly let his finger draw the imagined line from the building to the base of the statue where we sat.

He pointed at the sextant and then at the angled bends on the drawing's lines.

He'd overcome my stun. He was back and activated within his passion.

He was alive in the world of his vision. So was I.

From what I could figure, the man had used the sextant to plot the tops of buildings surrounding the spot where we talked. The radiating pencil image on the page was the cumulative pattern of their positions from this spot, as well as their degrees of rise. Each line's length was the distance from the spot. And the length of each bent end was the height of each building, with the angle documenting the degree, minutes and tenth from the position of viewing.

Using the building tops rather than the sun, he was able to use the sextant for setting up his own personal depth of field for this location.

And he'd done this all over the city.

As he showed me later, the other pages in his bags created similar 2D visualizations of other 3D locations that he frequented or just liked.

He was abstracting stereoptic vision into numerical data.

He was drawing statistical space.

This was his 3D.

How all this and his destroyed left eye related to what he called The Bible, I never figured out. I gathered he wasn't talking about the holy book, but rather some baptism by fire that once befell him.

It didn't seem that he wanted to gesture out that traumatic story for me, so I just let it remain unknown.

That story may have been too much for my drugged-up brain to handle anyway.

But, then, without any hint of segue or introduction, the man pulled out and showed me a faded, hardback photo book on Pre-Aztec architecture.

The book was what he'd been using as a pillow.

Entitled, *Our World in Color*, the book was one volume from an old American encyclopedia series for teens, showing architectural sites around the globe.

This particular book, with its scratched blue spine, was on the Popoloca ruins in Mexico.

He held the book up for me to see and it trembled in his hand, as though earthquakes were part of its design.

"You like this?" he asked.

I wasn't sure how to understand the question.

What did he mean by "like"?

57

He slid his thumb into the book's base like pitting a plum, and the pages split open.

With 1970s framing and color tones, the photos in the book were busy with accessory details: leaves and vines, accumulated rubble, pale tourists in white shorts.

All this busyness in the images conveyed a feeling that more was affecting things back then than affect things in photos now.

Now, each photographed object seems to be staged like a super model, set within a decontextualizing backdrop of abstract absence. Objects now seem to float in private voids with a Platonic dreaminess.

But, in the 70s, photographed objects seemed to be expected to bleed on each other more, perhaps like the humanity that envisioned and fashioned them.

"You like this?" he asked again and turned to a particular double-page spread of photos.

They were stone carvings of what the caption listed as Ndachjian-Tehuacan temple.

I knew about this place. I'd been shown pictures of it years before by someone who'd been to that temple and knew it better than this book.

One picture in the book depicted a large round skull. Its eyes and mouth were bold with vibrancy. The other image on the page was of a 1,000-year-old carved stone torso, its hands extending out of slits where another skin's hands hung slack.

I'd seen these other pictures before too. They commonly circulated through the skin trading culture. We'd all seen them.

The 1,000-year-old stone torso was a carving of a god wearing a human skin. An enlarged detail next to the photo showed how a tie closed the seam of the external skin that was being worn by the stone torso. It showed the ancient method of using a criss-crossing cord.

I was once taught how to use this traditional way of adjusting and securing a skin in place. It was standard practice to share such history with other skin wearers looking to learn. But I have long preferred to install a strip of Velcro in a skin. It's easier, cleaner and much more discrete.

Before Velcro, people used buttons and snaps. This criss-crossing cord method is only used by zealots of mythologies.

Was this right-eyed guy one of those? One of us?

Holding the book, the man began speaking in animated Japanese, his voice slipping from its previous delicate pace.

I watched as a loose and jagged edge between language and memory began to fray in him. I couldn't understand most of the Japanese he used, but from his repeated use of the words, "Xipe Totec," I knew he was talking about the ancient god depicted in the pictures. The Flayed Lord, as he is also known. I'd never heard that god's name spoken before. I'd only ever read it. So, I felt it was interesting that this man's pronunciation was establishing itself as the authoritative one in my mind.

Random chance making trusted meaning.

"You like this?" again he questioned, pointing at the pages.

I still couldn't tell what he meant by "like."

Was it about preference or similarity?

Did he wonder if I liked the book? Did he wonder it I liked ancient architecture? Did I like Pre-Hispanic art? Did I like the ancient practice of wearing skins?

Or was he questioning my degrees of similarity to the figure or actions depicted in the sculpture? Was he wondering about my own skin practices?

In general, I could confidently answer, "no" to most all interpretations of his question.

No, I don't feel a great interest in Aztec architecture, art or their myths of regeneration and fertility. No, I also don't wear skins over my skin, let alone skins derived from human sacrifices (although one could argue that every skin on the Internet that is available for sale or trade has been sacrificed by its previous user and offered to the unknown others who may occupy it). As well, No, I am not a priest, nor even a god.

Yet (just joking, haha).

I can only say that, "Yes, I like 70s photo books."

But, I didn't say so.

Rather, in response to his question, I playfully pulled back the sleeves of my jacket to show him Cadere's bare wrists, while saying, "No."

Then, I asked him, "And you?"

He looked a bit stunned and then laughed in a contagious little giggle that set me laughing along with him.

I didn't know why we were laughing.

Then, he said, "Good pillow," and we slipped further into a shared laughter. He pretended to sleep with it under his head again.

As is true with most experiences in life, I can't say I know what meeting this man means. But, equally, the power and value of the meeting are undeniable.

I couldn't live without it.

Even if I wanted to, I couldn't live without it.

The moment blossomed with an intensity that far exceeds any meaning I can try to determine for it.

We said, "Good bye" and waved each other away as friends would.

58

I reached the end of the Nakanoshima Garden Bridge, turned around and looked south. Standing atop the north bank of Dojimagawa (Nakanoshima's north river) and looking down along the glassy canyon of high rises, the buildings replaced the sky with their collective wall.

They bounced each other's skies back and forth. An infinity of repeating reflections.

The buildings also reflected the movements of the clouds in tones of polarization good enough for ad campaigns.

On such a day at such a time, when the clouds drift in such backlit beauty, there is a feeling of glory to watch the heavens reflected off polished office surfaces. The lines of glass and lines of metal and lines of glossy stone surfaces layer themselves into the transient whites and depthless blue.

I lost track of which were moving against which's vastness.

The buildings' tops felt like they were flowing away, with me pulled along with them in earthbound union. It was as though I could sense the earth's turn. The rooflines slowly fell back, receding to reveal the stable ever-presence of the heavens.

That human horizon against the forever.

This was a situation when the capitalized "Heaven" feels right. That by its sheer vastness, it can't not be the constant container.

Which it must be.

And on that day, as if in premonition or a burst of some pareidolian synaptic rain, the sky looked full of bulbous sheep.

I have always been the kind of person who enjoys watching the shapes and shades of clouds as they appear, change and become things I can unpredictably recognize. I then enjoy how they always become something else.

But this was the first time that every single cloud only looked like sheep. Massive and disproportionate, fluffy white and long past shearing-time sheep.

No alligators, rabbits, island chains or heads of hair on holy fire.

All the clouds were sheep, and then changed into other sheep.

Such moments of overriding absolutism always make me look for an external program that forces the restricted and exclusive outcome. And, while I thought that the last dose of medication I swallowed may have already passed through my system, I admitted to myself that there could have been some special side effects from the mix of various residuals.

Trace chemicals from the menstrual pills may have mixed with others from the asthma gas to create a new cocktail side effect that causes sheep-only visions.

With this as a qualifier, let me tell the next stage of my wandering.

Get ready for sheep jumping about within a localized sky and running the pathways of a non-scalular jungle.

59

By "non-scalular," I mean to say that the jungle didn't have the expected proportions that I think a jungle should. It didn't have appropriate scale.

Or something like that.

But, before I could get to the jungle and sheep, I had to get down off the edge of that bridge. And that was becoming kind of a challenge.

I was feeling compressed into a space too small for myself. My own density and scale weren't oriented right, causing uncertainty about what could and couldn't be possible. Causing nausea and wooky knees. Causing doubts about what's up and what's down.

I approached the north end of Nakanoshima Garden Bridge and looked down the stairs. It felt like a precipice.

I turned to my right and looked across an enclosed area of granite street décor. Bridge anchor, pedestrian ramp, river wall. As well, a massive concrete grain of rice was perched like a stylized sofa. More crappy city art.

Also, there was a small rock garden that suddenly seemed vast and moonscapey. Barren vistas and broken cliffs. While the garden was actually a miniature arrangement of jagged stone slabs, it felt like its distances would take eons to travel. This space's spaces refused to allow correct comprehension.

Something fluttered in my gut. I moved to keep things inside from spinning.

Jagged grey surfaces in the rock garden's ridge lines reoriented as I shifted myself. They moved in front of some surfaces and move behind others. Obscuring and revealing. Disorienting the stability of the rock garden's lunar lines. This prevented me from reading the edges of where one object ceased and another began.

I couldn't take much more of this.

I stopped, but my stomach didn't.

It had its own ideas.

My legs rebelled in response. They buckled and I flopped straight down hard on my ass, unbalanced and Humpty-Dumpty frightened.

What was up became down.

What was steady became shifty.

What was far became near.

All of this accumulated in ways that might be suitable as one of Alice's undocumented adventures in Wonderland. And similar to Alice's falling down the rabbit hole, in order for me to continue my approach toward the sheep, I was required to make an unsteady descent.

From my wobbly ass, I studied the best way to get down the stairs and off the bridge.

For much the same medicated reasons I have alluded to previously, my mind was temporarily already not quite right. I was too much of some things and not enough of others, influenced from both the outside and from within.

Details seemed too large and the massive shapes of the city seemed to be tiny particles of brevity. The prints on my fingers looked like canyons being run by rivers of sweat, but the expansive highway flowing above my head seemed like no more than a blip of reflection off a spider's thread.

Maybe the old man's "Bible" was now getting to me, reducing my 3D vision to a 2D view plus angle-data.

I edged a bit sideways and tilted my butt off the stone step. Then, I proceeded to scoot down the stairs with slowness and care.

I crouched to touch each of the stone steps with my rear end and a steadying right hand.

I used my colorful stick to probe the steps beyond and below me, as through to test the stones further down for their supportive density.

As I came to the base of the lowest stairstep, I looked across the street. That's when I noticed that a block of the city was over-flown with sheep.

Yes, over-flown with sheep.

That's what I said, it was over-flown with sheep.

Yes, sheep. In the air.

Ewes and rams were trotting about in the space above a square of pretty typical commercial property. Streets framed the tall boxy office building lot. Architecturally, the building was made of repeated white horizontal floor lines. Each floor of its 35 stories was spaced by a black gap of equal thickness, giving the structure the feel of a massive accordion undergoing a stretch.

A mass of expansion and contraction.

A big Polka exhalation.

But, oddly, within the space of this building and its property, sheep dashed and grazed in its sky.

I carefully sat down on the bottom step of the stairs to let myself sort out the sorts of things happening up there in that patch of Osaka's sky.

Weird and lively.

At times, the sheep would stand completely still in some particular spots.

Sometimes they were in pairs, sometimes in groups and sometimes alone.

But, then, suddenly the sheep would jump up as if leaping over a small fence and dash downward—or trot upward—across invisible slopes that seemed to give structure to that sky. There seemed to be sheep paths that were lost to my view. I could see the paths the sheep took, but not the paths they were on.

Also, the building that seemed to be there didn't seem to be there for the sheep. They passed through it with ease. But the various sheep dashing through the sky always stayed within the confines of the streets that framed the block. Those lines seemed to be their recognized and respected pen. Their territorial range.

I couldn't see any reason why.

But as I got to my feet and moved closer to the building's space, I had no doubt that something kept the sheep from exceeding that square, either some invisible sheep-dog, biologically imprinted limit or a fence of electric shocks.

As illogical as it all was, there must be something at work.

But I could not determine at that time what it was that kept the sheep in. And I don't know now either.

Regarding the limitations of what I could know, I'm just writing as a witness rather than promising to make everything make sense.

About other sheep stuff, I could later gain access. But, what limited the sheep to that zone is still a mystery. But something did. They never exceeded those street-line borders.

60

Anyway, the sheep obviously seemed to enjoy that secluded field of sky. They galivanted about and seemed to hope for no better activity than to just leap up and run about weightlessly above an urban Osaka City business block.

The sky was their idyllic, rolling hills.

I moved off the steps, stepped into the street between the bridge and the sheep's building, and then stopped. I just stood and watched the sheep from there for a long time.

When a taxi beeped, I moved further to see it all more closely.

At each step, I worried that it would all just vanish. I thought that if I passed some line too far or exceeded some delicate angle of the light, it would all go POOF and be gone. I worried it was merely the hallucination I suspected it could be.

But, as I approached, the sheep continued. The vision maintained. I could still see what was apparently happening there. Other walkers on the street would proceed into the square of the building's block and nothing would happen. Nothing would change. The pedestrians seemed as oblivious of the sheep in the sky as the sheep seemed to be of them.

As well, the sheep continued to move through the appearance of the building that occupied the block as though this massive piece of architecture was not there. The building didn't influence their movements in any way.

Watching these worlds layered over each other but not affecting each other kind of worried me. It felt like things were coming to a point of confrontation. Something would trigger a change. And I worried I would be that trigger of destruction.

Because I could see what logically seemed to be these mutually exclusive realities co-existing, I prepared myself for the spell to break when I set foot inside the square of the property and somehow shifted the balance.

I kind of believed I had that much power.

But entering that absurd convergence of worlds definitely seemed like the next threshold, regardless of the risks.

So, of course, I had to try.

I stepped up onto the sidewalk and stopped at the outer edge of the space.

I looked up the invisible wall of what I assumed was the sheep's limit, the line at where they would always change direction. I could see no ripple in the air or blur from some different type of vertical plane. The sheep just seemed to know how far was too far.

I took another step closer and still nothing changed. Still the sheep ran up and down the empty sky and passed effortlessly through the building that loomed over that area of the city.

But, then, when I finally proceeded into the square and passed the invisible wall's line, entering into the quadrant of the sheep's play, I could see otherwise than when I was on the outside looking in.

Within the enclosure of the sheep's world, what had been empty sky from the outside revealed itself to be a lush green world of a shifting garden that floated down from above and up from below. All of this greenery was beneath the prancing trajectories of the sheep. Inside the sheep's square, I could see that they were not just leaping over invisible fences. They were playing in a vertically shifting arbor which descended to the ground-level from the building's rooftop elevation, and then undulated back up upon ever-shifting slopes of grassy elevation.

The building was a vaporous blur amidst the ever-changing meadow land.

The hills were alive with the sounds of mutton. The grassy landscape was constantly rising up and dipping down in ways that resembled a slow motion green liquid sloshing in a jar. A botanical lava-lamp. Always responding and always responsive, the sheep and the ground were playing agile games of change.

The building didn't prevent this in any way at all. The building just vaguely remained as a vaporous solid.

Also, once within the sheep's world, I had to play along. I had to respond to the shifts of surfaces that then responded to my shifts. I couldn't merely be an objective and passive onlooker. I couldn't be an outsider. I had to run down and up the hills too. The hills used gravity to force such play.

The city block admitted me into that garden of alteration, and its effects were as real as a racing heart-beat and sweat-soaked shirt.

Why I was let in, I don't know. I don't suspect there is a rationale of blessing that merits it, but it was exclusive to me.

Other people—I could see—couldn't see it. They just proceeded along their pedestrian ways and moved amidst the human-made space that co-occupied the square of streets. The walkers went into the building. They rode the elevators and worked at their computers. They entered the first-floor café in the building that was surrounded by the shifting garden as it flew up to the rooftop and then dropped back down in its roiling flow.

I suspected that the sheep and rolling hills could be some effect of layered time, of the past asserting its duration into fibers of the present. But, again, I have no evidence to support that being reality anymore than the experience just being a very special augmentation of reality due to my day's worth of chem-cocktailing.

Just speculation.

All speculation.

But, then, who decides which way to reduce glory down to mere guts or gore? We each experience driving reality from behind our own pseudo-toy steering wheel and dirty windshield. So, I think we each get to tell of the journey in the way we understand it. We each get to make the maps. Beside, what does it matter? Nobody really believes anyone else's experience that much anyway.

61

Anyway, back to what happened with the sheep.

Running down the pathways of the floating garden, I would occasionally meet these sheep. And, while you might be imagining that this experience was kind of a new-age trip of fluffyfluffy feel-good, those sheep were not cuddly little Jesuses of kindness and docility.

They were massive and very fit beasts.

I'm nearly 6-foot, but they were almost that at just their wooly shoulders. Both the males and females. And they didn't have a vibe of domesticated farm dwellers willing to passively let some shepherd flip them over for a sheering or throat-cut.

They didn't welcome me as their human overlord or natural superior.

They confronted me with a sense that I had to learn equality from the hoof up, and if I was going to try and play the narrative of man over beast, I was not going to have their easy acquiescence. I'd have to choose to either demand their obedience with brutality and constant ferocity, or I'd have to try to rise to a higher level of equality between differents.

They were not going to be easy-going, regardless.

I had no energy for commanding the sheep to be mine, and no interest to stay long enough for that responsibility anyway. So, I just kept moving through that world that maintained them. I tried to not get headbutted or bit. I tried to not treat them like my idea of sheep.

Each of us were just beasts meeting beasts.

And each occasion of meeting provided the open context for everything possible between fight or flight. Life doesn't only offer those two opposing extremes, but rather a shifting groundwork on which we constantly reorient ourselves with others, and with other selves. We meet and we have a range of responses which we can repeat like rote or we can alter and experiment off of.

Each sheep was a fluffy, filthy-white void. I could not look into their eyes and fathom what any of them thought or even if they thought like I think I think. But, my ignorance didn't mean each of them didn't know what it was doing.

They each clearly did.

Why—as with myself—is a whole other level of unfathomable speculation.

But, in terms of how they responded to me at any particular bend in the paths in that garden of shift, it was obvious that each of them understood what they were doing. They were each responding to conditions without being remotely controlled by some triggering system of mere instinct or stupid-beast behavioralism. At least not anymore than such factors also influence my actions.

As well, in our meetings, the responses we had with each other changed. Recognition and experience and memories also influenced each of us. We became a small culture of familiars, but not long enough to build trusts, let alone "friendships," or whatever degree of intimacy a word like that might mean between sheep and a man in a used skin.

But, I did learn to respect them as individuals. We each had our own fears, curiosities and brief leaps into play.

62

I became physically exhausted in about 30 minutes.

I stepped out of the sheep block, got a can of coffee and rested on a street curb.

After getting back a bit of energy, I walked east.

I approached Midosuji again, the street I started the day on.

The Dojima River flowed slowly on my right. Between it and me was a fence made of graphically cast-iron ginkgo leaves.

Their gold-painted fans appeared to be floating along with the river's flow. The gold leaves were more proof that Midosuji was just up ahead.

I walked on a dark-tiled promenade that was raised both above the surface of the river and the level of a sloping street which led back down to the block of sheep.

Basically, I was atop a piece of Osaka safety infrastructure: a reinforced wall designed to delay flooding, which also doubled as municipal beautification.

But, the beauty aspects were aging. The path was showing differing degrees of decay and the scars of downkeep.

As with many public spaces, this one had had various temporary histories over its existence.

Assorted hints evidencing these histories were still present in this stretch of sidewalk.

How long these signs of Osaka's unremarkable history will last is hard to tell, but at least until some excess in the city's budget gets earmarked for the "aesthetic maintenance" of this area. Then, money will be granted to erase these markers of past moments. Then, the tangled lobby of construction companies, Yakuza and local labor will swoop in and transform this area, engaging it in the fiscal-year-end ritual where slush funds inflict seemingly random beautification upon the city.

Then, whatever area gets selected will be fenced off, torn up and reworked in the name of urban "renewal." What might appear to be a perfectly good park bench or a familiar stretch of sidewalk, will be switched out with a new version of what it was before.

Trees may be cut down all along a road near a station and then those very same plots of dirt prepared to receive new trees.

"Out with the old and in with the new," might be a nice way to rationalize it.

But the practice ignores the fact that spots have micro-histories and that the city's surfaces store moments for the lives of residents.

A small cherry tree might mark a link between two former lovers who annually noticed its special pattern of always being the first tree on the street to bloom. If the tree is cut down, more than its roots are pulled out.

The city is not merely a tool of urban planning and progress. Place is a hive of memories, its hum an intricately tuned tone of intimacy.

Why not just let trees grow, even if they push up their blacktop encasements?

I'm sure there are many logical reasons why not.

But I digress.

Back to the promenade I was walking on.

It was rather unique in how it had missed (for so long so far) the pattern of ritual renewals that the city inflicts. Obviously, the tiled walkway had experienced only the necessary repairs that would keep it from being a danger.

A crack in the flood wall was obviously fixed some years ago. A large black wad of industrial goop had been injected inside the crack and cured. That was probably a good thing.

A glass light dome had been replaced with one that didn't match its sisters.

A broken wooden strut on a bench seat was replaced with a plastic one that stood out in contrast to the weathered others.

The lack of unnecessary attention gave this area of walkway a nice quality of abandonment, an accumulation of shabbiness which preserved a richness of the location's signs of contact with different times.

The delicate scars of locational urban history remained like intimate ruins.

How the promenade achieved its shabbiness in a city that is devoted to keeping construction companies occupied perhaps relates to this riverside walk's origins.

This embankment promenade was built in the late 1990s, on the tail end of Japan's economic boom. But the area quickly became occupied by urban squatters who moved into Osaka from more viciously anti-homeless cities of Japan, such as Tokyo.

In the early 2000s, Osaka's public spaces became filled with street dwellers who erected semi-permanent temporary structures made of blue vinyl tarps that were carefully wrapped and tacked over frames of cheap lumber. The entire lengths of riverside parks and walkways became lined with these bright blue abodes, each house serving as a home for one or two, usually elderly, homeless men.

Perhaps the homeless boom was evidence of some neoliberal sequence of events that the unseen-hand of capitalism let "naturally" play out following the burst of Japan's 80s bubble of greed. As debt breathed inside of peoples' lives and began consuming them from within, companies commenced their legal processes of collection: letters requesting immediate payment, warnings of extra charges, threatening phone calls, late-night knocks.

As these passive-aggressive measures gave way to other legal procedures of conviction, wages were garnered and bank accounts were attacked. Crippling fines were added on top of interest due. Collateralized cars, boats and houses were seized.

A chase often inspires people to flee.

So, they fled to Osaka.

The general and specific mechanisms of delinquency commenced the endless assets-collection hunt and thousands of men vanished into the layered invisibility of Osaka's ever-welcoming streets.

63

I was told in 1999 that if a man can live on the streets for a week, he'll see there is no reason to go back to regular life.

There are systems and cultures at work outside of, and weaving through the gaps of, the incomed classes.

(But, in full disclosure, I wasn't told that by a homeless person, so who knows how accurate it really is.)

64

The riverside promenade I walked through remained marked with signs of times of homeless occupation. Both in stuff still in disrepair and in details showing through the subsequent touching up.

For example, readable patterns of grime and repeated use were deeply stained into spots on the brick tile work. A large glossy square of darker-tinted red tile glowed with newerness amidst the wider context of fade. The shiny square was edged by wiggling lines of black grit and rivulets of rain runoff.

These details revealed where a tarp-house had long shielded the tile from the sun and where collected rainwater had been channeled into off-flows.

Urban temporary architecture logistics.

Other examples I could find were textured patterns of new paint. The new paint covered particular areas of a previously painted pole. The paint's worming textures tell that the pole had long had ropes tied tightly around it. Those ropes had scored the original paint as their tensions changed in different weathers. The new paint added a layer to those earlier textures, but didn't remove them.

The old continues pushing through the new.

Pasts can't be forgotten.

What's hidden is revealed through what hides it.

Another painted texture on an electrical box showed spots where stickers or adhesive tape had been applied and later removed. The glue that remained collected dust and other wind-borne filth. The once-sticky undersurfaces left stripes and rectangles and circles and other shapes of rough texture layered under the overpainted surface.

Where not repainted, the gluey shapes remained. They become blackened attracters of dirt and any other drifting particles that tumbled on Osaka's gritty breezes.

Time is documented in these evident stages and processes.

The touches occurring on touches.

The expressions and the erasures.

Official or unofficial, random or natural, destructive, scarring or beautifying, all are allowed by the city's open acceptance.

65

As I walked along the promenade, I came to a section where the walkway veered right. This particular bit of tiled pavement extended out onto a concrete buttress reinforcing the river's wall as well as disturbing the course of the river for a short stretch.

The zag in the path led around a collection of exhaust-coated bushes and thin, winter-bared trees. This little touch of urban nature was in the process of bringing forth new buds for spring.

This brief offset in the path's line stood out, not only for actually sticking out into the river's flow. The location was obviously different. It was full of marks that had been left totally untouched by the city's diligent work crews. The site was a pristine accumulation of how the area had been used by someone—or some some—for some time.

The ruins were fresh.

The marks of life weren't erased yet.

It was like an isolated time-capsule of a street-squatter's existence.

How this spot had escaped immediate removal felt kind of miraculous. The zone wasn't even taped off yet. So, the history of the user was still all there.

Bits of bedding and traces of meals eaten rough.

Patterns of use showed where sitters had regularly propped themselves up against the embankment wall. The burnished patina of repeated leaning. The accumulated scratchings of countless outed cigarettes.

The space was laced with exhalations and conversations, fits of laughter and drunk arguments.

Someone had been recently dis-inhabited from the spot, but the smells, burns and smoldering embers of that life remained for my archeologizing.

This urban dig-site was still uncontaminated by those who would come to scrub it out. The beautifiers had not arrived yet.

And amidst the ragged detritus of someone who'd seemingly lived in this place for a long time, there was a particular object that fascinated and puzzled me.

I will tentatively call it an "art piece," because it was a sculptural form without evident purpose. But, also, I'll call it art because the object had that kind of energy of concentrated passion about it. It had that dedicated care of touch.

66

On a superficial and literal level, the object was just a big round wad of printed garbage.

It was a densely packed mash of adhesives and peelings from the city's decorated surfaces.

It was a collection of the city's acts of signage.

It was an orb, built of culled messaging. Discount coupon flyers. DJ stickers. Bits of old shop signs. All of this was layered and worked into the single form of the object.

The object inspired my scrutiny and contemplation. Partly for its size, but mostly for the mystery of its fabrication.

It was about 50cm in diameter, which showed that it was a sustained work by someone who took it seriously for a long time. It had endured a duration of effort. Whoever made it hadn't just tossed it into the river. Whoever it was had repeatedly returned to the work.

As well, while not perfectly spherical, I could see how the contours of the object's surface were delicately worked. The outside was meant to be more than merely its outside.

The object had been considered and cared for, but not meant to be some kind of allusion to something else. The object was not referencing some other or more meaningful bulk of curvature—like the Earth or a head or a mushroom cloud. The object wasn't trying to be something else, but yet it was completely built out of dead references—from points cards and peeled gummy branding. The object was made of product wrappers and book covers. It was made from innumerable stickers that had marked the city's poles, traffic boxes, bridge railings and whatnot.

The creator had stripped the city of its adhesive labels and used them as the layered patchwork of the orb's expanding skin.

This variety of thin, found materials were layered over layers over layers, and then evidently coated with some kind of hardening liquid, maybe some binding sheen of epoxy or super-glue.

And then the surface seemed to have been sanded or rubbed extensively in order to smooth and blend and polish the various adhered bits into the object's undulating roundness of dense messaging.

Wrinkles that had surely occurred from applying rectangular stickers onto the object's convex surface were worked into a ceaseless smoothness. Its smoothness gave the object a soft glow. A whispering sheen.

The object was a densely compacted sphere of the city's briefest voices. Osaka's temporal utterances.

Event notices.

Lost cats.

Temp-job ads.

Kids' characters.

Contest point stickers.

Plumber ads.

Hello, my name is.

Introductions to prostitutes, pimps and pop-bands.

Offerings of all the city's briefest meaningful urges.

67

The object sat in that discarded site for discarded people of a discarded time as though it was on display.

Bits and pieces of paper that were to potentially enlarge the object were packed underneath it, like thousands of tiny shims piled into a cushioning bed for the future they'd form. The stack of building materials raised the orb about 30cm off the ground.

Perched like a dare to gravity and earthquakes atop that mound of collected refuse, the orb drew my eyes into its centrality.

It captured me in orbit.

I approached carefully, and then crouched down.

I studied how it hovered there. I examined its impossible logistics.

Then, I pulled out a creased piece of slick paper from underneath it.

It was the folded cover for a music CD by some band called Plastic Mantra.

The cover's glossy surface glowed orange and red and gold in an odd polymorphous shape that looked like a tabla player melting into a sitarist. A critic's blurb of faux praise across the back of the sleeve read, "Osaka's finest fake Indian music duo."

I tried to slip the folded paper back into the stack of others, but it somehow upset the balance.

The orb seemed to shiver. Or quiver. Or maybe shimmy.

I pulled the paper back out and the orb preferred that. So I put the CD cover up on the embankment ledge.

I squatted in front of the object for about a minute more. Just looking.

As I was about to leave, I wondered more seriously about why the object was still here. How could it remain so delicately balanced atop this stack of papers? Why hadn't it rolled off or been kicked over? Why hadn't it been thrown into the river or even stolen?

I touched the orb lightly to see how carefully it was balanced. To test it a bit, or perhaps secretly punish its patience by "accidentally" knocking it over.

But it didn't budge. It was steady and solid.

I pushed harder, but nothing.

I tried to lift it and check its weight, but it was too heavy for me to lift.

It couldn't be made of just paper, I thought. There had to be something else inside. Otherwise, it was up to some trick.

I gave it a solid shove and tried to push it off its stack, but again it resisted confidently.

Obviously, it was fixed in place somehow.

But, then, what was the shiver I saw it give before?

I grabbed the CD cover off the wall and wedged it into place again, and again the orb appeared like it was ready to topple.

I touched it and the object began to slowly turn from my hand's contact.

It spun and spun, way too long for moving just from my touch.

I watched it rotate.

I let my fingers drag on the object's surface, but it didn't slow at all.

And, even though I pressed down with enough pressure to flatten out the pads of my fingers, there was no sensation of friction and no slowing of the orb's rotation. It was as though my fingers were touching an exterior that didn't affect the visible layer at all. The object just kept turning without registering any cause beyond my initial contact which set it in motion—or at least I assume it was my touch which started it spinning.

I really don't know.

I tried a few other things to stop it, but nothing changed it. Its spin actually seemed to get a bit faster, but that's hard to be sure of too.

I pulled the Plastic Mantra cover out again, but nothing changed.

I put the CD cover back up on the embankment wall and it was quickly picked up by a wind and tossed into the river.

Oops.

68

The weird object reminds me of a folk tale someone told me, about a king who was brought from the capital to see a sphere that hovered above the ground without reason.

The sphere could not be grabbed or moved or affected in any physical way.

It merely hovered about a meter up in the air next to a small river. The sphere hovered there as though it was waiting for some agent of context that would come to realize or reveal its purpose, some hero of a future who would arrive and provide an unimaginable answer.

A new reason to believe.

Until then, the sphere's situation was unknowable.

So the king was called to come and give judgement because all the villagers who had seen the object had gone insane, unable to make it make sense in their world.

Some advisors told the king that the orb was from God, but others said it was from the devil.

Finally, the king came to see the object himself because the sphere undermined every logic held in common by the society.

The king, in his wisdom, ordered it to be covered with a cloth and posted 4 blind guards to continuously keep people from removing the shroud.

The king gave no answer for what the object was. The king could think of no other solution to save his people. But he too eventually went insane, staring into a palace mirror that he'd gradually scratched through to its wooden backing.

69

I left the spinning orb and continued walking beside the river.

Just before reaching Midosuji, I passed by a crowd of smokers in a zone of tobacco quarantine.

Most of them were bouncing slightly to keep their bodies warm.

A line painted on the ground and a series of yellow knee-high poles formed the edge of their smoking limits. Their physical movements were restricted to non-mobile knee-dips and some waist-twisting.

Gotta keep the blood moving.

The posted rules prohibited the smokers from moving amidst the rest of us.

But the smoke didn't care. Non-humans are often outside of our control.

The formalities of the smokers' limit-lines and poles seemed to be more of a punitive gesture designed by city marketeers to placate recent updates in TV-taught social moralities. The restrictions seemed likely for use in city PR campaign photographs touting how Osaka embraces international standards regarding the quality of urban living.

Anyway, the puffing-people voluntarily hemmed themselves into their wall-less pen. They played their symbolic role as the latest version of the THEM who should be publicly shunned. The sacrificial lambs.

Not talking, joking or mingling. Just dutifully smoking.

Observable outcasts by choice.

I watched the rhythm of their fingers moving back and forth between their faces and a rusty coffee can that was wired onto a filthy steel pole.

They bounced, sucked and tapped off their ash.

The glamour of the publicly flogged.

The smoke and scent moved in clusters of spread and drift.

The signage declaring limits and prohibitions didn't address or prevent that fact. No language for talking to smoke.

And, I could feel Cadere's nostrils get eager. They contracted and reached for that world of smoke. His nostrils reacted with spasms of quick sniffing, and I could tell they were dialing in their desires. They wanted to feel the textures of their old patterns.

His nose longed for the acrid and tinctured rush, yet again.

In response, I pinched my stick under my armpit and opened my blue bag of medications.

I took out a foil pillow of digestive antacid granules and tore a small hole off its corner.

I inserted the opening into my left nostril and gave a quick snort. Then did the right. Each sniff lifted some of the medicated dust from the package and set my sinuses into a brief sneeze-fit.

Mission semi-accomplished.

70

I turned right and headed south on Midosuji, crossing over Oebashi bridge which spans Dojima River.

A bright yellow boat loaded with tourists rumbled under me, its diesel exhaust percolating the water aft.

The bridge brought me back onto Nakanoshima Island. The final arrival of my day.

The sidewalk ran next to Midosuji Boulevard, between Osaka's tarnished-green treasury building and Osaka City Hall. Up ahead, on the edge of the sidewalk, I saw a pair of glowing neon blonds standing behind a portable metal table.

What were they pitching?

Arranged in several low stacks on their table looked to be various small booklets that they were trying to promote, sell or distribute. From where I was, I couldn't yet tell what the texts were about.

The pair seemed to be well organized, but not an organization.

They had a hand-made air about them.

Were they political? Religious? Social? Scam?

I stopped at a distance and tried to suss their purpose, position and approach.

I'm always interested in how ideas are pitched to people who don't really care.

It's hard to rope in people in motion.

People moving on the street have a special power to effortlessly dodge and schluff off much of what might try to cull them. Walkers can redirect their gravity away from what might try to draw them into an unwelcomed orbit. They have abilities to tune the flow of their attention and trajectory within the ever-shifting arrival/departure that is pedestrianhood and this gives them unique powers to glance off of and skirt confronting energies.

A walker has a toolbox of tactics that can be immediately deployed. From the various gestures indicating "Too busy" or "Sorry, I'm late," to the existence-evaporating refusal to make any eye-contact at all, walkers ply the currents of tangential commitments. They have so many ways to imply "fuck off" and redirect.

Therefore, a Street Talker is a peculiar breed in the world.

To talk at people who aren't really there to listen to you is something like befriending characters in a film. Your audience can ignore you in their private script without feeling any guilt.

And so, I always try to study street talkers. I try to learn by examining how their rhetoric succeeds and fails with people passing. The dynamics between a speaker and the passing audience reveal details about both the culture a message is being presented to and the people doing the presenting.

Thus, instead of going too close to the blonds, I held back. I watched and analyzed how the pair worked the flows of souls.

71

The two blonds were dressed in what might have been their different notions of a shared uniform. Autonomous fulfillments of a vague abstraction.

The man and woman both wore black pants and black sports shoes, but above the waist they were quite different.

The man was in a thick orange blanket-coat buttoned up to his neck. A graphic vertical block.

The woman's jacket was thin blue vinyl with a vivid yellow stripe down the left sleeve. Its thinness made it ripple almost like a fluid as she gestured and moved. She was the talker. She also wore dark oblong sunglasses that gave her something of a movie-star-from-the-colorized-film-era vibe. The sunglasses echoed certain curves in her cheeks and jaw.

The man's face was undecorated by glasses or facial hair, just dazzling white eyes casually scanning the world.

He had an intricately coiled nest of blazing blond hair stacked high atop his head. It occupied almost an equal space as his face.

Quite tall, he stood stock-still. Mostly silent.

His slender black fingers supported the edges of a large electronic tablet screen.

The glowing glass rectangle leaned against a section of his chest, his orange coat framing its graphic impulses.

His main job was evidently to propel the screen's illustrated narrative in sync with cues signaled by his shorter partner.

As she spoke, his finger would calmly swipe the screen and bring the next animated image into view.

The woman's dynamic approach was a model of contrast to how the man's minimalist energies silently advanced the visual elements of her speech.

While also a vividly blazing dyed-blonde, she was a compact motor of verbal energy.

Her hair was short and sharp, a wedge of head confronting the moment with language.

Her accent was hard to parse. Either a London English tweaked by Osaka Japanese, or vice-versa. She thrust her voice out into the pathways of passers, capable of tripping them up with outbursts of phrasings and questioning hooks.

Thought bombs tossed at the parading public.

"Who were you 10 minutes ago? How do you think you got here?" the woman questioned.

"Your choice to take this path sacrificed all those other options along the way. Eliminated the chances for those other selves to be there or there or there. Existence depends on such violence."

"Yeah, who was that back then?" Her tall partner's voice reinforced her point as he flicked the screen onto a colorful caricature showing a long line of old men moving amidst mountains.

"Did you follow someone here? Do you feel safe 'cause you did? Part of a big plan? Do you know where you're going because you're part of some well mapped whole?" the woman continued probing.

"Naw, that won't work," the man countered on the theme.

"No, we arrive at this moment lost. We're born lost, every step along falling into the world from bloody loins. No other way possible, despite the abundance of sign boards, and street names, and arrows."

The man flipped the screen to an image of a thick book of maps, each page showing the same city. An animation started. The book's pages turned and with it the place's names began changing changing changing in an accelerating series of location-identity blur.

He said, "Where are you from? I'm from NewTroitCagoAngeLeans."

"Place is Trace. Face is Trace. Space is Trace," she announced.

"You can't taste what you ate yesterday," the man commented while flicking the screen to an image of an animated woman in a well-stocked kitchen hungrily trying to feed herself from an empty bowl. Her oversized spoon repeatedly dipped into the bowl, rose up empty and poured nothing into her mouth. She licked her lips beneath a thought-bubble reading: DELICIOUS!!

The blonde woman behind the table lifted up a booklet and slightly sang, "Nothing exists, and everything proves it!" Her voice cascaded across the words in melodic shapes.

From my position near the road, I could read the pair's rhythms and methods.

I dissected how they would first get the Midosujians' attention with a challenge or confounding phrase. The bold-lined cartoon images on the screen would draw a glance from walkers while reinforcing the verbal hook with some bait.

I noticed how eye-contact with a pedestrian would be followed with a directed question to engage the passing individual's specific situation.

Then the partner would reinforce a comment or question with a quick confirmation. This would reassure everyone that the blond pair knew what they were talking about, that they had a shared message to share.

This was not a random fishing expedition or just a bunch of rants. The pair had a strategy to split the pedestrian swarm into individuals and then engage them as two blonds against each lone walker.

Divide and concur.

72

I shifted my position a little bit to get more of a view of the pair's table.

It had a thick orange cloth draped down the front which reached almost to the pavement.

The words Radical Atheism were stenciled across the cloth in blue paint. Definitely handmade, but also well made. It showed skill and care.

A perfect and unrepeatable one-off.

Holding the small white booklet up like a card of surrender, the woman went into long form lecture mode:

"You won't survive this moment unscathed. You can't. But that's not a fact to simply inspire fear. Sure, the fear is real, but that's not its only limit. The fear of death is also pointing at a sublime fact. It's showing why you can live. Not in some big God-nod of right/wrong behavior for admission to heaven, hell or some feel-good bait-n-switch that fits you in as a cog in the orbits of BigBang stardust. The fear's answer to 'why?' is much more intimate and immediate. It's the process that your life directly depends on. The fact that your survival is not certain—that nothing's is—is why life can happen. It's life's survival method. If you or anything could maintain a state of unchanging purity, nothing could live. The fact that you and everything is open to being lost is what makes each thing possible to become. The dynamic aspect of life would be impossible without this."

"All this brutal brevity," the man poetically summarized.

His tablet screen seemed to get caught in the midst of a chaotic static of glitches.

Pixelated colors ate at themselves and each other, frazzled lines and boxes of digital deconstruction appeared, vanished and flashed epileptic codes.

But, for all the tablet's apparent wildness, I sensed it was programmed to do just that: an intended image that hinted beyond intentional imagery.

A programmed mistake.

An invited ghost in the machine.

"You would have never come into being without the violent demise of something else, of others. None of us continues without the ends of other entities, without things coming apart and giving us this chance to be. Each thing can come into being because each thing can also be exhausted. And if anybody tells you their god or logic system can protect you from this finitude, or that their program can fit you sweetly into some big-picture immortality, then you can know they are running a scheme on you, trying to turn your most primal and accurate sense against you. They are playing your survival fear against you. Reducing it to something superficial and feel-baddy. They are trying to make you hate life."

"Defend your life," the man echoed.

"Your fear of death is a sense of sublime accuracy about your specific existence. About being now and here. Your fear of death is the accurate fact of being nowhere. That feeling you've learned is fear is the awareness of the moment. It's what NOW feels like. It's the vehicle that suspends all surety and facilitates life's potential to pass away or become new. That feeling is a sign of life's open structure, of its desire for entangling complexity. It's of of of. And that feeling is not merely fear. It's richer than can be named. It's life of of of."

"Ghosts aren't afraid of dancing with destruction. Are you?" the man questioned.

"Am I afraid? You're asking me? Sure. But, I also must say, 'Yes' to being afraid. I must confirm it with, 'Yes.' I don't have any other choice, really. I can't refuse it. Even to say, 'No' is a way of saying, 'Yes.' None of us can do otherwise. We are always already in the embrace of life," the woman responded.

The man swiped a super high-speed time-lapse film into view.

The film showed the growth cycles of plants, birds, humans, trees, mountains, planets, political parties, historical eras, hemispheres on the earth, etc. Each stage vanishing and giving way to the next and next and next.

"Being relies on an autoimmune condition of of. Of being of others. Life's self-destruction keeps life going. Life eats of itself, perpetually. Life feeds life with life. Unlike theories from theologies, histories or science systems that offer you a sense of immortality within their absolute notions of universal purity and grand-scale completeness, the temporal finitude of being is not something we hope to overcome. Temporality facilitates being."

"Nothing exists, and everything proves it," the man echoed from earlier in their lecture.

"Even the concept of Nothingness can't save you. You are always already slipping into lostness. We all are."

"We all are," the man repeated.

"Here, in this moment-by-moment togetherness is our chance to offer care on equal terms. Now and here—in this nowhere—we can be real. For this long. For as long as we have. For now. Caring for each other now and here is salvation. We salvage what we get, make use of what has been lost. Not in some big scheme of assuaging fear, but in the direct sharing of fear. In the shared uniqueness of experiencing this fear alone with others. Alone, with others. Together. Together, we are lost and willingly saying, 'Yes' to futures."

By coincidence, a large truck for collecting blood donations passed by on the street behind me. The man at the table held up his hand and waved. I assumed his wave was towards the truck's driver, but, in fact it was directed at me.

Strangers greeting strangers.

73

"Hey, André Cadere. Come say hello," he called out.

Suddenly, he'd become the voice reaching out into the distance. Was he trying to hook me in. But he was off their script. Or, he was going unscripted.

I felt a bit shocked and exposed, but I walked over to meet the pair.

"I was thinking of getting that skin, too," he said. "It was up for sale for quite a while. Right? But I decided to stay in this one. So, that skin must be pretty recent for you. How's the fit?"

He could read the mix of complexity and hesitation in my eyes.

"Probably a bit uncomfortable. Right?"

"Yeah," I said. "Its get-to-know-you stage has not been so smooth."

"I hear ya. Change can happen quick, but getting used to it is what takes some time."

"Very true. And Time's slow horse is named Discomfort."

"Haha. Nice," he laughed and got a quick glance from his partner. "So, I guess, I'm glad I gave up on that skin. It'd be tough to get that one to fit on me."

"Very true. It'd be a big stretch."

By this time in our exchange, I could feel the woman's eyes growing impatient behind her sunglasses.

"Is she in a skin too?" I questioned.

"No. Hers is just hers. She's got enough going on inside there already."

I reached out to shake her hand. She kind of complied, but seemed uninterested in becoming conversational, or even casual. Her work mode maintained.

I picked up a couple of their small white booklets. One was titled, "Autoimmune Finitude" and the other, "Affirm the Time of Survival." Also, I took a photocopied article by Martin Hagglund called, "The Radical Evil of Deconstruction."

I put a donation in their box and said, "Good luck with what you're doing. But, can I ask, why don't you use Japanese? This is Japan."

She curtly answered, "He will."

"What she means is, we switch. You just saw the English version. Later, here or down by Tsutenkaku, I'll do the Japanese version. She's got a Chinese one in the works, too. Who ever knows who's lurking and listening, and why? Right?"

"Very true."

"Anyway, I better let you go so we can get back at it. Hope you enjoy the reading and work things out with the skin. It looks good on you. Actually better than in the Amazon pictures."

"Thanks. See you."

74

I moved further down Midosuji and leaned against the pedestal for a bronze sculpture that had gone very blueish green. The art work on top featured a group of seven miniature children playing on a sphere. An earth for sharing. Our blue marble of chemically patinaed bronze.

I thumbed through the Radical Atheists' texts while I waited for nothing in particular.

Glancing through pages, I wondered if I had accomplished anything in my Terminalian drift.

How to measure it if I had?

How to measure if I hadn't?

I'd set out in the morning to readjust my relationship with this skin. It was now the end of the day.

Rather like any other day.

Things had occurred.

Were they earth shaking? Mind altering? Physically transformative?

No, and yes.

I could dial in reasons for either of my No/Yes conclusions, and both would only show me how I weigh, define and combine things. My reasons would tell me more about me than about my day. More about how I think than what I've done.

There was no denying the day.

Mundane or radical, things had taken place. How could they not?

Reasons are built with their retorts baked in. Each is a limit implying contexts, assumptions and doubts. Each is a handle presumed to be useful for controlling change. Each has a center that cannot hold.

So, maybe the undissected day should be enough.

But it never is.

Whatever never is.

The questions arose again. Had I fulfilled my plans? Did the drugs have their effects? Were the outcomes all to my credit or blame? Did the various worlds I came into contact with remake me in some new and meaningful way?

Yes, and no. No, and yes.

And, and, and and and.

I flipped through another of the little books and came to a page with a large black rectangle. It looked like a full-page redaction of whatever was intended to be there. But I didn't know if that's what it was for. I didn't know if hiding something was the purpose. It could have been a printing mistake. It could have been a symbol.

It could have had a meaning.

The page offered a question without a context or hint. And it quickly became my favorite page in the book.

I stared at it for maybe five minutes.

I read pages before and pages after the black rectangle, looking for some explanation or logic. But there was nothing to conclude its meaning, or its goal, or its part in a method.

Questions and ideas whispered in my mind. The sibilant little language of self returned.

The page spurred me to respond. I wrote in my tiny-scrawl across the white space margining of the redacted section. The misprint. The void. The symbol. The rectangle.

When my notes stopped, they looked like someone had walked barefoot next to the black blank.

My penned notes radiated out from the rectangle's edge. Jottings of imagined logics and their tempting tangents. Quick sketches for an essay or an article. For a film or a piece of music. For a discussion series. Each one, something to be fleshed-out later.

Each a promise to things I know I will never do.

But, that's my practice, I know. My broken oaths to such texts are part of my working process. My fodder for my larger failures.

I climb inside the skin of someone else's thoughts and intentions, to see how I'd live their life. To see how things would go wrong otherwise. To find out how ideas would turn out differently with me as their meaty motor.

I want to occupy their skin with my customs, habits and urges.

This book is an example of what can result.

75

Tiring of the Radical Atheists' booklets, I slid them into my blue bag. Additional drugs for the pile.

I crouched down at the foot of the sculpture's pedestal. I leaned back, putting my weigh against what held up the world. I waited that way for maybe 10 changes of the crosswalk light, and then I moved over onto Yodoyabashi bridge.

Standing at the wall spanning the Tosabori River, I looked at the flow of greenish water and the flow of walking people and the flow of traffic heading south.

One of the booklets' titles popped back into my mind.

I took out, "Affirm the Time of Survival" and started reading it.

The whole thing was something of an introduction, and I could feel my urge to make notes start spinning again.

I dug around in my bag to find my pen again.

As I started a note beside a section on how Derrida connects hope with affirming the moment of survival, a group of people began gathering on the bridge. A man with an envelope passed out some ragged pages, and the group members began reading to the car traffic.

I recognized that this was the same group of people I'd seen several hours earlier doing something outside the toilets at Utsubo Park.

Now, they were here and reading strips of texts to the passing vehicles. They were reading a fluttering script of taped-together texts.

With my pen hovering over the margin, I watched and listened.

I couldn't figure out what or why they were reading, but I liked it.

It didn't feel like they were trying to make meaning or trying to convey a message. They were doing without trying.

Their recitation to the traffic seemed less about answers and more about inciting questions.

I felt there was a connection to the Radical Atheist blonds who spoke English at the passing Japanese walkers. But what was the connection?

Was this group speaking to people locked inside machines of blur?

Were the blonds doing the same?

Like the saxophonist in the morning, were they all listening for some new sound the city might send back?

Were they trying to slip human words and logics into the murmurs churning around them?

Were they trying to hear how the mix of their multiplied voices altered vehicles in motion?

Were they playing games of chance within this unceasing change and flow?

Afterword of Before

This story started on February 23rd, 2018: Terminalia.

On that day, I joined the *3rd Annual Widdershins Osaka Walk* and walked the specific route through Osaka City that is documented in this story. During the walk, I carried a colorfully striped stick rigged-up to a portable sound recorder and captured audio textures that I found along the way. I took the walk with a goal to playfully document sounds of the city's bumpy and crunchy and spongy and slick surfaces.

Alone in a bar after the walk, I listened to the recordings and wrote notes so I could remember what the sound textures and their locations had been. In that act of listening and note-taking, pieces of the *Terminalian Drift* story first appeared.

In the time of writing *Terminalian Drift*, I told myself—and others—that I was working on an "experimental text." I think this was partly a way to save me from the writer's-block-inspiring pressures of writing a "novel," but also it was because I'd never written a work of prose in this type of place-reliant way. It is common for me to write poetry inspired intimately by the place and situation of the poem's creation, but I'd never done this for a longer and more sustained work. My poetry is usually composed in one sitting and draws extensively on the specific place and happenings within that context. In this way, my poetry serves to creatively explore and commemorate a specific and often mundane moment, endowing the text with the reality of the actual place/experience and also augmenting the real with the poetic imaginative. In my poetry, place becomes entangled with perception, and vice-versa.

Thus, writing *Terminalian Drift* was an experiment for me, to see if I could use my poetic methods for a longer work of prose. I wanted to see if my site-specific poetic approach was versatile enough to extend to a larger area. I wanted to see if I could layer a wider area with my poetic territorialism. As well, I wanted to see how this type of poetic interaction with a wider city area might alter or infect me with the city's narrative energies.

I approached the writing as a collaboration with the specific places, times and happenings occurring on the February 23rd walk. I committed myself to drawing on things that happened in those places at the times I was there on the walk as the architecture sustaining the story. Within that armature, I would let my imagination drift and fill. I saw my job as to imaginatively document, respond to and augment the reality of the walk. So, I think of *Terminalian Drift* as a work of blurred fiction/non-fiction documenting/augmenting specific events in those Osaka locations on February 23rd, 2018.

As mentioned, *Terminalian Drift* was inspired by and derived from joining the *Widdershins Osaka Walk*, which was part of a world-wide series of walking events generally linked via the *Terminalia Festival* (https://terminaliafestival.org). Terminalia is a celebration of the ancient Roman god of boundaries: Terminus. Exploring themes of boundaries and borders—from the geographic and the bodily to the experiential and the sensuous—obviously plays a big part in the story via the main character.

To give some specific credit, the *Widdershins Osaka Walk* is a Situationists-inspired *dérive* designed and facilitated by the Osaka-based Welsh artist and researcher Gareth Morris Jones. Jones' annual *Widdershins Osaka Walk* project traces a course through contemporary Osaka City by overlaying a map of six boundary stones ringing the medieval city of Leeds, England. Jones' *Walk* also employs various creative activities (including readings, performance and games of chance) via which the walk's participants engage its locations and disrupt their habits for experiencing urban spaces.

My writing of *Terminalian Drift* was also partly inspired by Phil Smith's mythogeographic ideas and practices.

Also available from Triarchy Press

Ways to Wander the Gallery
eds. **Claire Hind & Clare Qualmann** ~ 2018, 80pp.
25 ideas for ways to walk in and beyond an art gallery.

Ways to Wander
eds. **Claire Hind & Clare Qualmann** ~ 2015, 80pp.
54 intriguing ideas for different ways to take a walk - for enthusiasts, practitioners, students and academics.

Walking Art Practice: Reflections on Socially Engaged Paths
Ernesto Pujol ~ 2018, 160pp.
A book of reflections from a monk, artist, social choreographer and educator – for performative artists, art students and cultural activists .

Walking Bodies
eds **Helen Billinghurst, Claire Hind, Phil Smith** ~ 2020, 340pp.
Papers, provocations and actions from the 'Walking's New Movements' conference (University of Plymouth, Nov.2019)

Walking Stumbling Limping Falling: A Conversation
Alyson Hallett & Phil Smith ~ 2017, 104pp.
An email conversation between the authors about being prevented from walking 'normally' by illness.

Walking's New Movement
Phil Smith ~ 2015, 98pp.
A guide to developments in walking and walk-performance for enthusiasts, practitioners, students and academics.

walk write (repeat)
Sonia Overall ~ 2021, 92pp.
Sonia invites us to see walking as a creative writing method and sets out a particular form which she calls walking-writing.

The Pattern: a fictioning
Helen Billinghurst & Phil Smith (Crab & Bee) ~2020, 208pp.
A handbook for exploration, embodiment and art making. Describes the secrets of 'web-walking'.

The MK Myth Phil Smith & K ~ 2018, 192pp.
A novel for decaying times set in Milton Keynes.

The Footbook of Zombie Walking
Phil Smith ~ 2015, 150pp.
Despair, climate change, zombie films, apocalypses, city life, walking & walk-performance… *"a very fine book… I recommend it to everyone with an interest in walking-philosophy"* **Ewan Morrison**

The Architect-Walker
Wrights & Sites ~ 2018, 120pp.
An anti-manifesto for changing a world while exploring it.

Rethinking Mythogeography
John Schott & Phil Smith ~ 2018, 52pp.
An illustrated upgrade to the principles & practice of mythogeography.
"…ideas spin in high frequency, creating a shadow walk more vivid than the real one." **Mary Paterson**

On Walking… and Stalking Sebald
Phil Smith ~ 2014, 198pp.
Phil describes a walk he made in Suffolk in the footsteps of W.G. Sebald and sets out his approach to 'conscious walking'.

Mythogeography: A guide to walking sideways
Phil Smith ~ 2010, 256pp.
The book that started it all *"mocks and subverts traditional expectations … in a field where silly concepts are written of with gaunt severity."* **Journal of Cultural Geography**

Guidebook for an Armchair Pilgrimage
John Schott, Phil Smith, Tony Whitehead 2019, 144pp.
"It is wonderful - a brilliant idea, beautifully done, with a sweetly companionable tone to the writing." **Jay Griffiths**

Enchanted Things: Signposts to a New Nomadism
Phil Smith ~ 2014, 98pp.
A photo essay focusing on signs, simulacra, objects and places that prove to be more, less or other than what they seem.
"…you'll find our cities and countryside ripe with hidden meanings, visual puns and unintended contradictions…" **Gareth E Rees**

Desire Paths
Roy Bayfield ~ 2016, 142pp.
"Roy Bayfield rises from the dead and re-discovers walking as a way of life... a fine mythogeographical grimoire." **Gareth E Rees**

Covert: A Handbook
Melanie Kloetzel & Phil Smith ~ 2021, 110pp.
30 movement meditations offer a straightforward, embodied practice that can defend us against invasion in the everyday world.

Counter-Tourism: The Handbook
Phil Smith ~ 2012, 228pp.
"Heritage sites would do well to take on some of his ideas, especially those on multiple meaning and injecting fun into visits." **Museums Journal**

Counter-Tourism: A Pocketbook
Phil Smith ~ 2012, 84pp.
"Buy the book! I love Mythogeography. A whole new take on the world. Always fresh. Great way to shake loose entrenched forms of heritage tourism." **Prof. Barbara Kirshenblatt-Gimblett**

Bonelines
Phil Smith & Tony Whitehead ~ 2020, 362pp.
A dark novel set in Devon's Lovecraft Villages.

Anywhere: A mythogeography of South Devon
Cecile Oak (Phil Smith) ~ 2017, 366pp.
A vivid portrait of a small part of South Devon... An adventure, momentous and fleshy as any novel. It is also the first, detailed mythogeographical survey of a defined area.

Alice's Dérives in Devonshire
Phil Smith ~ Foreword: **Bradley L. Garrett**, 2014, 216pp
"I have found every possible excuse to creep away and read it... how beautiful, bewildering and breathtaking it is." **Katie Villa**

A Sardine Street Box of Tricks Crab Man & Signpost
(**Phil Smith & Simon Persighetti**) ~ 2012, 84pp.
"a terrific resource...a handbook for making a one street 'mis-guided tour'." **John Davies**, author of *Walking the M62*

www.triarchypress.net